# BENEATH CATSEYE

## PATRICIA I. WILLIAMS

## Mythical Legends Publishing

Sale of this book without a front cover may be unauthorized. If this book is coverless, it may have been reported to the publisher as "unsold or destroyed" and neither the author nor the publisher may have received payment for it.

*Beneath CatsEye* is a work of fiction. The characters, incidents, and dialogs are products of the author's imagination and are not to be construed as real. Any resemblance to actual events or persons, living or dead, is entirely coincidental.

A Mythical Legends Publishing Mass Market Paperback

Copyright © 2013 by Patricia I. Williams
Published by Mythical Legends, 2013
Publisher@mythicallegends.com
http://mythicallegends.com

ISBN-10: 0962783536
ISBN-13: 978-0-9627835-3-1

Printed in the United States of America

**9 8 7 6 5 4 3 2 1**

## DEDICATION

To God and James

PATRICIA I. WILLIAMS

## ACKNOWLEDGMENTS

To Wikipedia – wonderful source of knowledge
And to everyone who pursues their love in science fiction, in writing or film.

http://www.bbc.co.uk/cymru/cymraeg/yriaith/tudalen/welsh_phrases.shtml

http://simple.wikipedia.org/wiki/Welsh_language

http://www.cs.cf.ac.uk/fun/welsh/LexiconEW.html

http://www.wordgumbo.com/ie/cel/wel/we.htm

http://translate.google.com/?hl=en&tab=TT

http://www.last-names.net/origincat.asp?origincat=Welsh

http://www.wordgumbo.com/index.htm

# Stalled

Fleet Admiral Pryor, Generals Spaulding and Panos stood shoulder to shoulder staring out the observation deck clearsteel window. They were the old guard, the last of the military leaders whose origins was Earth itself and not the depths of space. It had not been considered they would live to see the arrival of the colony fleet to its destination.

Below them rotated the disaster they had traveled light years to occupy. Air and soil not quite right, violent unpredictable weather. They would have to do additional terraforming and hope the ships held together long enough for the place to become more viable. They dared not land. There would be little logic in that action, even though many were clamoring to be free of this confinement. At least in space they could shuttle between vessels and send out the smaller survey ships to map the system and mine the shattered sister and its fragments for metals they would need to maintain their position. Expeditions could eventually be sent below to get better readings for an estimate of how many years it would take before people could actually live on Haven.

Admiral Pryor did not know who had coined the name, but it was certainly inappropriate. There was no haven here, no home for the hundreds of thousands of souls the military was responsible for. It was up to the scientists now. They needed some hopeful news for the colonist regarding how long they would be denied walking in the distant light of this sun and having land beneath their feet once more. He did not want to think about the star being older than their home star or the planet for that matter. Would there be any descendants to see the future end or would history repeat itself?

General Panos considered the dark clouds racing across the planet. What views the satellites had been able to garner showed very few bodies of water of any size comparable to Earth. Command had lied to them. The military leaders of many countries had rounded up the unwilling to live alongside others desperate for a chance to live a better life on a frontier planet. Many wanted away from the corporations and military that was vying for rights to the whole Earth. The others were dissidents because they still held religious beliefs of one kind or another, were radical politically, or worse, violent in the pursuit of their goals. Frankly, Panos was considering a mass execution to eliminate some of the possibilities of future insurrection. The others would not agree, but he saw no reason to allow hard core terrorists to intimidate the law abiding people once they made planet fall. It never made sense that Earth packed them off instead of executing them. Genetic diversity was bullshit when compared to being killed in your bed. All he could see occurring was a race of nutjobs who might one day discover the means to return to space.

General Spaulding's grim expression did not bode well

for any negative feedback from the scientists. The General's ex-wife had recently come to the lead scientist's attention and regrettably, some thought, they were reviewing her research. Spaulding hated the woman with a level of bile he barely controlled. Some of the Colonels had already approached Panos with their concerns that he was less than stable. The Fleet Admiral had been placing more responsibility for Spaulding's operations in the hands of his subordinate, Major General Keresztes. Spaulding appeared unaware.

Right now they had a fleet wide crisis to prevent. Food production and oxygen levels had to be dealt with first. The doctors and scientists had to come up with a way to keep the people orientated to living on a planet when they had been and would be, born and raised in space even longer than planned. He knew the next few rotations would be a headache. Thank goodness his personal staff was loyal and obedient. Fleet Admiral Pryor was a excellent example of a leader and did not defer the hard decisions that had to be made over the rotations. Panos hoped he would see reason to at least eliminate the worst of the offenders. For the sake of survival they could not afford to have so many in lock down and resources pulled from the citizens to keep the scum alive.

General Spaulding scowled. The damn scientists were going to be allowed to experiment on the damn planet. He did not see any reason to bother. The entire trip was a dead end. Better for everyone if they resupply, repair and continue on. Be damned if he would settle for the chaotic life of the planet bound again. Instead of remaining in orbit and playing god with the environment below, they should leave. Nothing good would come of Sandra getting to influence the damn egg heads dicking around with the planet. This was going to be nasty business.

He would get his chance to speak at the staff meeting later today. Perhaps the colonists should be given more input. They could not possibly want to remain orbiting an unlivable ball when the limitless expanse awaited them. His own grandson had no interest in a planet and the general was in full agreement.

Spaulding had survived the purges and upheavals of what life had become on a planet. On the ships there was structure and hierarchy that kept things running smoothly. Responsibility was in every individuals hands. He had no desire to go back to babysitting a world of helpless civilians and spilling blood in the dirt. Ideology was essentially crushed under the demands of keeping life support intact. Any mistake out here was death. That threat was the best deterrent for abhorrent behavior.

He remembered old Earth history when certain regimes fractured, a few countries gave up stable infrastructure and decent family life for ancient ideologies. Neighbors killed neighbors, raped and pillaged. Humans had spent centuries killing over skin color, religion and gender differences. He knew all these things would start again if they settled on a planet. Sandra had wanted the chance to prove science would amend these problems. She had proposed genetic engineering to create a more amiable human. Her experiments got her arrested, imprisoned. He divorced her because her beliefs were sick and testified against her. As disgusting as humanity was, mindless drones obeying their scientists masters frightened him more. Who knew he would wind up on an outward bound fleet of undesirables destined for death in space and the bitch would be in stasis on the prison ship. Spaulding scowled.

# Long Live the King

Campfires were burning low and in the big tents the wounded slept in drugged oblivion to their pain. Within the largest tent, the nobles of Daear gathered around the cot of their king MeekBlade. A hastily erected tarp separated the deathbed from the entrance to the tent. The pallets of the dead and deathly wounded Cadre were scattered there, faithful even unto death. Bloodied sheets and thick pad of soiled bandages lay strewn around the feet of frantic Healers. In the dim corners behind the cot darker sentinels hovered, waiting. At their King's command they had left his side, for he and they knew all effort was useless. The Barons watched the Palace Healers struggle to bind the King's wounds against hopeless odds. The lances had struck thrice in his belly.

His guards had fought until they died. A sneak attack from two squadrons of the enemy wearing Daear's colors overran the King's observation post before further help could arrive. Even now Vidor's brother StraightBow struggled for life on the other side of the tarp. The old man confounding the odds once again, fighting to survive punctured lungs and snapped ribs. He stood alone over his King's body fighting the last of the attackers, as a bloody froth filled his helm. MeekBlade had refused to flee and leave his men to fight without him, proving that what many said about him was indeed the truth. He was Cadre first and always, King was an afterthought.

Baron Vidor grimaced in sympathy as the king struggled to push himself upright. The man's face was soaked in sweat, his fair skin leached of all color. His dark brown eyes were overflowing with tears and blood had soaked his Cadre braid an even deeper black. The healers propped pillows and blankets around him even as they worked to keep his intestines bound inside his body. Vidor's armor was covered in ichor as well as Baron Caddock and Baron Meinrad's. They had not quit the field until messengers had ran through the troops carrying the white flags with the red crosses that meant the king had fallen.

Baron Colwyn and his brothers, Gavin and Nardo, arrived. The latter in his perpetual state of intoxication. Baron Renfrew sat on a low stool with his sons Haul and Trahearn at this back. Their presence caused some level of bemusement in the midst of this tragedy. There were few fools willing to cross swords with the man, let alone attempt to kill him. His family was renowned for being expert warfarers at their most vicious. Haul was expressing profound sadness and was hard pressed to contain his tears. He had a strong regard for the Cadre King.

Here were the most land rich of the elite, who traced their bloodlines back to the first days on the planet. Lesser nobles crowded the entrance to the tent and spilled into the mud churned street of the tarp city. All of them were proven to carry the genes of the First Admiral and First Generals in their bodies and no less than three of their many children were Gifted in some way. Only Gavin and Renfrew had the bright auburn hair that gave further indications of their dual heritage.

All of them wondered as they stood in the torchlight who would wear the crown. MeekBlade's wife had died a few rotations after childbirth and his only child was a mere eighteen summers, a delicate and refined young lady that was the joy of the court.

MeekBlade had not refused the drugs the Cadre Healers had administered, knowing he could not die screaming in the agony that found him once his breastplate was removed. He spat the blood that pooled in his mouth into a cup held by one of his remaining Cadre in the field. The young man, Runner, was covered in bruises from his own day spent in battle. Tears spilled down his dirty face at the loss of MeekBlade, for the King was one of the Cadre's own. Exalted to the throne by the death of his distant cousin, King Edmond who died without wife or issue. Runner would not break down however, he must stay by the King's side until the end.

A flurry of activity had the Baron's reaching for their swords, when the tarp was flung back. Princess Riayn rushed into the room shoving them away so she could see her father. Her guardian, Talon, pushed them further back by the sheer breath of his shoulders. He covered her back, even in the healer's tent where all should be secure.

Meinrad frowned and spat on the ground, his temper ill served by the battle and the coming struggle for the throne. Here was a chance few would see again. Since his last wife had died he was in perfect position to marry the princess if her father so decreed.

Caddock shook his head in sympathy. She was too delicate to be here on the field, but MeekBlade had never left her behind if he rode into a skirmish since her sixteenth summer. Of course she was surrounded by Cadre guards, with Talon many times restricted to her side. But still it was hard for the Baron to imagine so sweet a child having to see her parent die so horribly. He shuddered as his thoughts touched upon his own children, relieved they were behind the metal gates of the Citadel. They were not here, dressed in ornate bright blue and silver armor, fit only for a parade on Union Day, watching their father suffer a long drawn out death.

Vidor had only wanted to prevent her from seeing the horror of her father's bloodstained body, but Talon was commanded by no one but the princess and her father.

It had been a bone of contention for many rotations that the Cadre did not take orders from the masters of the elite families. To many it seemed arrogance and even more so when the entire troop went to their knee before MeekBlade on his coronation. Never before had the Cadre bowed to any, King or commoner, but no member of the Cadre had ever been King. If the Cadre had been loyal before, now they were fanatical in their zeal. There would be no quarter given on tomorrow's battlefield. The remaining members would demand retribution.

Riayn caught herself before her body fell upon blood stained blankets and pillows that wrapped her father's brutally damaged body. Her eye's fell into his pained gaze and she knew he would not survive his wounds. He raised a shaking hand and she eased down beside him and grasped it to her breast. He struggled to speak and when one of the healers would have admonished him, Talon's armored arm pushed her away. The Barons were wont to protest, but the unveiled hard gaze of the protector challenged them with drawn blade. Caddock shivered. He could not endure looking into Talon' eyes. Spitting once more into the cup, MeekBlade drew an agonizing breath and addressed his only child.

"The Citadel is yours to guard my Queen . . . my Cadre to . . . to . . . your hand . . . I . . . decree. No challenge. . . Queen . . . my Queen."

The Barons were stunned, and some outraged, but Talon had not flinched. His steady blade held them away and kept them silent.

MeekBlade's knowledgeable gaze flickered to the elite of the lands that surrounded his death bed, noting even now how some of them could not hide their bitter faces. His child already knew who to trust, who bore watching and who might need to be maneuvered into betraying their true intent. He had taught her well and honed her Chosen into the most relentless killer the Cadre had ever produced. The remaining Cadre were already hers. She had grown up in their arms, played on their training fields and obtained her own mount among their ranks one secret dark. He dared not leave his land of Gifted and 'pure' human in the hands of his barons, loyal or no.

There were those who would change the status of the Gifted if they could, make them slaves, deny Chosen to keep them weak. If he could have avoided this fate, he would not have left his daughter for many more rotations. But he could rest in peace knowing she was as strong as he could make her for the coming battles. He accomplished much to keep the balance of his kingdom and the world.

Blind fools did not realize if the strongest Gifted fled these lands, in three generations they would revert to what they were when the humans arrived and eventually die as a race, but not before killing as many humans as possible. The loss of their genetic material would weaken humanity and make them vulnerable to the still poisonous world they shared. Even the humans who considered themselves pure were not so much thanks to the long ago geneticist that worked to inure men to the world. Division could not be allowed to occur. Death would be the outcome for all, yet still the mad ones insisted on the purity of humanity, foolishly blind to their own doom. MeekBlade could not stop the deep shuddering breath his body demanded. It hurt more than he could endure any longer. He pressed Riayn's hand to his bloodied lips and raised his tear filled eyes to the men surrounding his death bed.

". . . your Queen . . . I declare . . . it." It might be his last words. For long moments not even the crackle of wood burning in the pit broke the silence.

". . . I declare it. Riayn is Queen." Caddock's words ripped the barons from their shock and the group stared at the man as if not comprehending his words. The baron's scarred face and curly grey beard were soaked with his tears.

"I declare it. Riayn is Queen." Meinrad's words were rife with sarcasm, his lips curled in an habitual sneer, as he threw up his arms in exasperation, but the words were loud and clearly spoken. He might not have the crown, but a trusted adviser could still make his way, just more time and effort had to be expended. The others stared at each other or avoided gazes to hide their various emotions. Riayn never turned to face the barons. She was lost in her father's grinding pain and pride as he held her hand to his lips. His affection was still a bright sun in her mind and she reveled in its warmth.

"For pity's sake, allow the man to die in peace. Riayn is Queen. I declare it," snapped Nardo, raising the flagon of ale that almost never left his left hand. He threw the silver vessel into the flames of the pit and rushed from the tent. How could they stand to watch a man die in such agony and deny him this last wish? The poor girl would be pressured into marriage right soon anyway and the endless war would continue until they were all corpses. Nardo began yelling for his servant to bring him another measure of ale before he was anywhere near the tents of his family. Men at arms moved to avoid his wild insults and swinging fists, knowing it would be quite a while before he was drunk enough to pass out. Their King was dying and this once they would forgive Baron Nardo his tendency to strike with his fist when liquored up, which was a constant.

Inside the tent, the enormity of what the three Baron's had done was just now breaking through the shock that had stunned Vidor and Colwyn speechless. Riayn was Queen of the Citadel. Queen over the valley and the mountains they laid claim to. This child woman, not yet wed, not yet seasoned had the reigns of power in her hands. What would become of them?

Talon turned to face the stunned warriors. He did not speak to them, just watched as they flinched or ignored his gaze. MeekBlade would soon be no more. He felt the resolve of his Chosen and was prepared at this moment to ride into battle if so ordered. Riayn sighed as her father slipped from her mind like tumbling water into a drain. She was loath to allow him separation, but rejoiced that the relentless ache he suffered since her mother's loss was easing right along with the pain of his wounds. She held the memory of his relief as a cushion against her own loss now. She sobbed as she pressed his stained fingers to her lips and place his hand over his heart. She allowed herself only a few moments for tears however. She looked at Runner's brimming eyes and placed her hand against his cheek. The young man finally gave way and sobbed openly, clutching the goblet in shaking hands. He cried out loud and the word spread quickly across the encampment. The King was dead.

Riyan dabbed at her tears with a silken kerchief, blew her nose and tucked the soiled cloth in her sleeve. One deep breath and she rose, stepping past Talon to face the Barons.

"Hear me Barons of the Citadel. My father is dead, but we have injured in the camp that must be moved immediately. Send two armed patrols to protect them and send winged messengers to the Citadel for more to meet along the way. See that guards are set to protect those we dare not move. And make sure every other able bodied soldier is ready to attack before dawn, then get to your own beds. We will have services for MeekBlade when all return to the Citadel."

"My lady, we will take care. You need not concern yourself." Vidor exclaimed. You should return to the Citadel where . . . "

Riyan appeared as fragile as the Helleborine orchid

which survived only in paintings derived from the records of long lost Earth. Vidor was about to discover different.

"Do you question my authority Vidor?" The question was spoken in Riyan soft tones, but a shiver crawled stealthily up the Baron's back like an ice worm.

The Baron's eyes widen and he looked directly into the new Queen's startling topaz eyes! He heard Caddock's shocked gasp at his back and the creak and rustle of metal and cloth as the other men stirred. The innocent brown gaze of Riyan was gone and in its place gleamed the evidence of power, power held back behind an implacable will that would not be reined in any longer. Vidor reeled under the influence of that gaze. But Riyan did not ensnare him, her gaze flicked to each man in the tent.

"I expect all of you think my father erred in judgment, considering the extent of his wounds. You believe I will sit idle while you attend me in my grief. We have no time for grief. The enemy knows my father has fallen. I am sure Fredric will not hesitate to move on our position before first light to press his advantage. Prepare yourselves! We dare not be caught off guard." Riyan turned to the grief stricken healers. "Leave my father and attend those that need your services more. The Cadre will prepare a pyre for him immediately. I will attend his cremation as quickly as it is completed."

Surprise marked every face and Riyan sighed heavily.

"We have not the time to spend in farewells. His body must be immolated before the first of our people go into battle. Our grief must wait for memorials once we return home. Quickly! You think the enemy will sit idle as we wail to the heavens? Move now!" Power stirred within the tent. Fire erupted in the pit. The sudden flare up and sparks scattered the Palace healers. The shadows moved to the fore and the solemn Cadre Healers, made quick work of the stained bedding and prepared the King's body for cremation.

The Baron's fled the tent with her commands ringing in their ears. They did not acknowledge the joyous laughter that echoed across the camp from the Baron Renfrew. In the whole of her life Princess Riyan had only expressed the weakest of talent, to communicate with Gifted. For coils sake her eyes were brown. Her hair was a thick ash brown and she was so slim she bordered on fragile. Now the hair on their bodies stood up and the first of the shock was wearing off. The Baron's had felt it, the deep thrumming in their bones that sang of great power unleashed in their presence. It stirred the trampled earth and tiny green shoots of llygredd sprang up to begin their writhing journey along the stakes and ropes that supported the dead King's tent.

Riyan turned her attention to the weeping Runner. She went to her knees and spoke softly to him.

"It is time Runner. You must anoint the troop. We must make ready."

Choking down the sobs, the young warrior looked into his Queen's golden eyes and took from her the strength he needed to bury his grief until they were no longer under threat.

"Aye my Queen it will be done as you say," he whispered.

He shook himself and lifted the cup he had been clutching between mailed fists to the Queen.    She dipped fingers into the blood within and pressed them to her lips, tasting the blood of her fallen King again. Runner nodded and they rose together to face Talon. The Chosen dipped the fingers of his hand into the cup and tasted the blood of his fallen King. Runner removed the glove from his own hand and did the same. He struggled a moment to put it back on, but managed with the Queen's assistance. Then took the cup from Talon and passed it before the Cadre Healers before quitting the tent. All around him soldiers, healers, Gifted and Barons bowed as he passed making his way through the tent city to the camp where the remaining Cadre waited to taste the blood of their King. When CatsEye was covered by wind driven clouds, they would slip into the dark to wreck vengeance on their enemy's forward guards. When Fredric's forces moved in the pre-dawn they would not find their creeping spies nor attack a sleeping camp.

# To the Rescue

Harsh wind battered the highest crags of the Citadel's dark mountains, shredding the mist that usually kept the towering gates from the naked eye when viewed from the first checkpoint at the bottom of the pass. It moaned and whistled through the decorative iron arches all along the steep road to the apex. Worn by time and the elements, the wall prevented falls from the tunneled roadway into the deep ravines and crevices that light rarely touched and no man ever ventured. The capricious gales protected the entrance to Daear, but without the wall everyone, friend or foe, would be plucked from the road and smashed on the rocks below.

The icy eddies stirred the flames guttering in the metal fishnet bowls of the castle torches. The light from these ancient five-foot scones embedded in the vast walls reflected little off the company of stygian clad warriors and the damp blocks of aged metal and grey stone. Their armor was dull, absorbing the low light, with plain helms topped by flowing topknots culled from the feathered tails of their mounts. The soldiers were silent, the thrum of the wind a sort of meditative background to their intensity of purpose. A few of them swayed, caught in the rhythm of the chill breeze as they waited.

The equerry stood by, a critical eye on the dozen apprentice squires, who saddled and packed the victuals and bedding onto the broad backs of the Pegasors. This intent group of boys and girls hoped to one-day ride as one of the Queen's Cadre and an error in preparation when warriors would most likely see battle was not to be tolerated, nor the shame endured. They strained and grimaced, pulling the cinches tight and using all their weight to shift the recalcitrant animals so they would not be crushed between them. Pegasors had sharp claws hidden in their wide, feathered paws and fangs that slashed if one was too slow. Even their mane and tail feathers could lash out and leave fine lines of blood on the unsuspecting.

One of the tests was to be fleet of foot and observant. Too many scars could very well prevent advancement into weapons training and an ignoble return to civilian life. Rough blew jackets protected them from the high wind and mittens from the same material covered palms, but left the fingers free to detect wrinkles in the finer woven saddle blew and the leather bridles and cinches. The majority had their hair shorn to the scalp, a mark of pride for those seeking the arduous won status of the Cadre and to discourage hiding any wounds from the trainers. Many had a scar on cheek and body from the edge of the Pegasor's ire. Talon had won his war name the night he tamed his mount, coming away unmarred from a severe contest with the stallion he now rode.

Her self's personal guardian, Talon stood off to one side, his height and breath of shoulder lost within the deep shadows of the towering walls. Occasionally the flames reflected his hazy silver blue eyes, which thick black lashes usually hid from view unless he wished it. He appeared blind at certain moments. Many Palace Healers debated how he could see through the mist-shrouded pupils and why the aberration occurred. They were never allowed to examine or test his vision. He always reacted coldly even at the suggestion. One of the lads shivered and ducked behind the bulk of the war stallion, fearing less the unsettled temperament of the animal compared to the chilling blank gaze of the Queen's Own.

Like the deceased King, Talon was taller than average and large boned, with a muscled physique that marked his family lines as nearly pure human. It was said he was devoid of any magics, and the court had been surprised when the King had approved his appointment as guardian to his only child. Many wondered if he was some bastard relative or worse, some new horror bred for an arcane purpose. He did not have written family lines and never spoke of his life before coming to the castle requesting service. Of course, proof could never be found for the numerous speculations. The majority of the royal court considered him dangerous and ill mannered. Many had never heard his voice and few risked his attention for one reason or the other. He wore an unadorned golden ribbon in his black braid. It had been given to him on Presentation Day by the then five-year-old princess held in her doting father's arms. It was frayed with age and delicate, but the guardian took great care, entwining it each morning with his own hands through the black ones of the Cadre, each one blooded denoting his rotations of service. The night before Talon had gone after the Pegasor stallion and won his name and permanent place in the Cadre. It had been a triple celebration. All other tokens of valor lay in the man's trunks, only worn at demand of the sovereign on Festival days, his braid vibrant with jewel encrusted red and silver edged black ribbons.

Now Talon was morose. That set the tone for the other nineteen grim faced warriors sliding swords into scabbards and bows with arrows to their backs. A number double checked rigging that supported the sharp edged lances on the saddles. The warriors would assuredly discover what delayed the emissaries from King Fredric, which should have arrived two dawns past. Their Queen had stirred from her inner apartments to command them recover her future husband and his entourage. They would not fail. The civilians of both lands hungered for respite.

The wide golden topaz eyes of the Finder twins sparkled when their hypnotic gaze captured someone. Their heads were high, noses searching the wind for scent even before they could leave the high cliff walls of home. Auburn hair defied braiding and ribbons, curling away from confinement on its own. Confirming their status as having more blood of the indigenous ones who occupied these lands before the humans arrived. The hip length filaments quested about their shoulders in constant motion owing to their excitement. The pair's skin was unmarred by blemish of any kind except for a light tan due to their outdoor life. The closer the blood the more quickly healed was a truism that the more human fighters could appreciate. The fine boned young men fairly shimmered with their magical gift, leaving one of the women to place herself between them and the working squires less the children become distracted by the allure that magic ability seem to have for the more susceptible.

QuickStep's blond hair was tightly braided with the single black ribbon worn by a new Cadre admission and one jeweled golden one, a gift from the two she would now forever guard with her life. Her eyes were brown and she was not quite as head blind to magic as many believed, but that was a secret between her and the ones she protected. The twins were the only overtly gifted in the Cadre, rare indeed to find such there, as the stronger the magic usually the more delicate the physicality. But these men were deadly accurate with stiletto and arrows. It was rumored their hair choked the life from enemies at will. They were called Strike and Shadow. People were repelled as much as they were attracted to the twins. The Finders were always fending off marriage contractors seeking to add their bloodlines to families seeking better position in the hierarchy of the ruling class. Even though Cadre members never left until they died, and never contracted so a child could be held hostage.

Finally the youngsters surged away from the Pegasors and lined up before the equerry. The old warrior limped past them, his staff held in a tight fist, to check each mount with his own gnarled hands and still sharp brown eyes. He was dressed in the same dull armor minus helm, his braid heavy with jewel-encrusted red and black silver edged ribbons. The faded red ribbons were his badges of honor for he had served the royal families from the time of the King Idris, close to one hundred rotations ago. He lay down his arms after MeekBlade was laid to rest. He wore a kingdom's ransom of precious stones in his grey streaked earth brown hair. StraightBow was still recovering from wounds received in that last battle against Fredric's rabble. She, who he loved as a daughter, had entwined the new ribbons into his hair as the Healers struggled to save his life. They remained, stained with the blood of her father and her own minor wounds. Each of the Cadre bowed as he passed them, for StraightBow was still formidable, even though he strode without weapons and bandages could be seen at the edges of his breastplate. Few, with or without gifts, had been so long lived.

He stepped away from the prancing mares and single stallion, giving Talon a quick nod. All was in readiness.

The children ran off to pack away the unused items and clean the Cadre quarters in preparation for their return. Their exit abruptly ceased when the distant wrought iron doors onto the terrace opened. The Queen passed among them with her surprising soldier's stride, several of her attending women hurrying to keep up with her. The spires of her crown flickered, casting light about her person. Frothing waves of the pale ice blue gown floated about her ankles, the exact color of her Chosen's eyes. Her self's five Cadre bodyguards moved silently in the shadows at the edge of her radiance, prepared to strike with lethal response to any perceived threat. She was sending her guardian away from the palace. All of them would die to protect her in his stead.

She smiled at the children. They smiled in return under her shimmering topaz gaze. Her ash brown hair was pulled back at the nap of her neck and braided as her Cadres. The hip length braid bore the freshly blooded ribbons of the recently rededicated troop. Stones of various colors decorated the ribbons, a tradition her father began but now including gifts from each surviving member to honor her bravery and command during the last battle. The Cadre christened her BrightLance on the field and she refused to use her birth name from that moment. She would not soon forget the sacrifice of the twelve and would honor them always.

The court was appalled at her refusal to forgo the ribbons, no matter the occasion, as was proper for a young maiden. She honored her father's legacy in all ways and took pride in the Cadres devotion. She carried a jeweled short lance with crystal like blades embedded in the shaft, in lieu of the staff her father had always carried at court. It was the same one she used with deadly efficiency the day her father died. The new decorations deceived the eye of civilians. The Cadre would make sure their Queen could protect herself at all times. The jeweled hilt of the concealed knife pressed against her thigh was attached to a wicked barbed blade. Her dress had been designed to make the reach for it swift and sure.

StraightBow's staff struck the stone parquet and the children ran off to their duties, released from the enchantment of seeing the Queen close enough to touch. Her waiting women held back at the last, uneasy at the presence of the warriors and their fierce mounts. The soft pastels and bright summer hues of their gowns were illuminated by the Queen's crown, a vibrant bouquet shimmering within the dark. The six women, varying in age from a rosy cheeked twelve summers to grey haired matrons in the winter of their life, accompanied the Queen when she would see the squad of men and women off, regardless of the hour. They rarely had the opportunity to observe her interaction with Talon and the court was always desperate from gossip about the mysterious man.

Members of the two squads snapped to attention. The Pegasors huffed at the rainbows shimmering before their eyes. Talon stepped forward and went to one knee. BrightLance stroked the shorter ebony curls that were springing up, quite stealthily, from the head of her Chosen to curl around her fingers. His opaque gaze lifted to rest upon her face and her smile lightened his heart as it always did. He knew she shared all that he felt, all that he was and totally accepted him as she had from the day he walked at her father's side during his interview to join the squires.

He still remembered the whip thin tiny girl, three summers old, that toddled out from beneath a flowering bush to frighten her father. Only to collapse in giggles when the King dropped to his knees begging to be spared with much arm waving and pleas for mercy. The King had lifted her up. Then she noticed the grim child standing to the side and two steps behind the King. Shimmering gold enraptured the boy. "Mine!" Riayn shouted so loud her father startled and almost dropped her. "Mine", she insisted and flung herself through the air and into Talon's arms. She would not be removed. The King called the trainers immediately. The boy's head was shorn right there in the garden. To his secret shame Talon wept after it was done, an agony he did not truly understand until rotations later, meeting the most revered Gifted ones at court.

Talon slept at the foot of Princess Riayn's bed. He endured the periodic shaving of his head and learned to live with the constant pain. He was drilled by the most talented and brutal of the Cadre. He dare not fail any test because he was the destined protector, the one a Gifted needed to survive, the one who would serve her for all his days. It was a heavy burden for an orphaned boy who had only seen twelve summers and was also too intimidated by his surroundings to ask the questions which would have spared him rotations of pain.

The reasons for Talon' pain lay within a near lethal symbiotic relationship which began so long ago much of the truth is shrouded in legend. A few human scientists realized the Llyncu were genetically compatible and could ensure the survival of the human population on their new poisonous world and perhaps stave off the predator's own extinction. The human military units and their colonists landed unprepared for the very real dangers previous automated survey missions were never accurate enough to detect. The new planet was already populated, with deadly predators and rarely observed intelligences whose eerie shimmering gaze called many a human to a prolonged agonizing death in their coils. Unable to hunt the creatures successfully and with no hope of assistance from their distant command, the humans eventually won through fear and revenge to communicate and the Llyncu understood well enough to forge a shaky peace. To ensure something of themselves remained into the future of their tragically altered world, Llyncu gave up their DNA to be entwined with the invaders.       The horrors produced in the labs those first days were destroyed and no records kept. The truth was buried by time and forgotten in Daear, except within the halls of The Cidital's sovereign and the training halls of Healers and scientists. Only the legends remained for the general populace, romantic drivel to entertain folks in the taverns. But the separatists remembered and avoided the demons if they could.

Now Talon would bring home the enemy prince who would bond with his Queen and sire descendants to rule jointly over Daear and Haven, that is if the treacherous haint did not attempt to kill her bringing war once again to the miles high cliffs of Daear.

"Spare yourself worry beloved. I will be quite safe. I fear this prince may have met with misfortune and his father would cast the blame at our gates. It is said that Fredric does not regard the life of his own bloodlines with any higher esteem than one of the Gifted. Do this for the sake of us all."

BrightLance caressed his strong face and watched his eyes roll back and his breath release with an almost silent moan. As always her touch soothed him past meditation and created a deep pleasure that vibrated his bones. Rotations of endurance prevented Talon from crying aloud. He would not be unmanned before his charges for pain or pleasure. Her touch communicated her affection and devotion, released his worries and left him serene in spirit and satiated in body. In all his rotations here, Talon had graced no one's bed.

"I am yours to command my Queen. We will not return with empty hands." Talon deep voice rumbled too low for any of the women to make out his words. He stood and kissed each hand before they stroked over his shoulders and chest and the Queen stepped away.

Talon put on his helm, checked his weapons once again and climbed into the saddle. The stallion roared in anticipation of the hunt and fought Talon' hold on the reins.

He was kept to a walk down the winding terraced parquet to the guard stations below the Citadel. The remainder of the troop fell in line behind him. QuickStep held a guiding strap threaded through the bridle rings of Strike and Shadow's Pegasors, to keep them from racing ahead. The twins were so very eager the men riding on each side assisted to keep them pinned, avoiding the pleading fiery eyes that would enthrall them. The twins loved a hunt of any kind and were not above using their powers of persuasion to flee into the dark.

The Queen was a distant glittering beacon framed in an arch as the troop quit the last metal wrapped gate at the bottom of the road. They traveled very quickly and were soon lost in the barren rock. Their mounts leaping over boulders as there was no trail to the lower elevations. Eventually they passed beneath the ragged drifting llygredd vines, bare during the winter of the deadly spines that poisoned 'pure' or hybrid to various degrees. The vines hovered above them in clusters, sometimes whirling about in the capricious wind. The Pegasor's nimbly avoided stepping on fallen desiccated remnants of the barbed spines even in the dark. They produced a horrid odor if crushed underfoot. During the summer new spines covered the yellow airborne vines preventing invaders from braving the highlands. The spines were sensitive to vibrations and always injected any living creature blundering into their territory.

The troop did not make first camp until well into the evening of the following dawn. They had entered the twisted version of the old earth pine forest. It was full of bramble firs, warped pine trees and various deadly foliage of one kind or another. None of the large serpents common to the forest trespassed on their camp. The presence of the twins caused them flee the area.

***

Farrell shivered violently even pressed into the wet needles and debris of the forest floor by the warm heavy body of his guardian. Lucan had warned him that any sound would bring their hunters down on them and Farrell would not be granted a quick death. Lucan's body armor bruised him but the man's distaste was the worst, battering at Farrell's empathy and causing his own self-loathing to rise until he was nauseous. Crippled by fear, Farrell could hardly remember the joy he experienced those first days of anticipation when father announced he would allow the protector to return after so many rotations. He had dreamed of the boy who tried to save him from Mason and the guards for so long. Only to meet a man hardened by shame and war. Convinced that Farrell was somehow unclean.

The revelation that his protector loathe the sight of him tumbled Farrell into his deepest despair. He was unresisting when dressed in tattered blew and pushed into an open wagon to leave the estate grounds for the first time. He saw nothing. The first growth of his dark red hair was covered in a cowl that also shielded the soldiers that comprised the escort. He understood from Mason that he was being given as Consort to a demon! Mason laughed and jeered about the deal that would supposedly unite the kingdoms and end the war. The war Fredric, and his father before him, pursued until their country was riven with empty homesteads and impoverished villages.

Farrell did not understand how this could be since his father always said the demons must be destroyed. His brother insisted this Queen thing would not keep any agreement when she saw the weak and useless specimen that was insult and provocation rolled into one. Farrell was completely confused at the words by that time. He continued to shiver. He had peeked at the grim blond haired warrior that rode next to the wagon and remembered the one short-lived day of joy he had experienced in all his twenty summers.

Escaping his drab quarters, the eight-summers-old Farrell had been wandering alone in the kitchen garden when the fair-haired youth had stumbled across him. Lucan was the gardener's apprentice-son walking about to acquaint himself with his new workplace. When he saw the frightened child cowering at his feet, he spoke softly and attempted to ease his fear, thinking he was the child of one of the other servants.

Hours later Lucan was found holding Farrell securely and refusing to leave his side. Then soldiers had come with Farrell's older brother Mason. They snatched the young boy from Lucan's arms and made him watch as they beat the youth to bloody rags for bewitching the apprentice with his cursed yellow eyes. It was rotations later that Farrell was told Lucan had been shipped off to the forest borders and made a soldier, fighting the vile magic users that lived beyond the mountains. Vile magic like the kind everyone said he inherited from the duplicitous 'pure' woman the King had taken as second wife. None in her family were aware that in the distant past their ancestors had been subjected to the first gene therapy attempts at mixing human and Llyncu.

When his son was born undersized with shimmering

topaz eyes and stirring auburn hair, Fredric lost control and killed his wife on the birthing bed before he could be dragged down. His advisers convinced him that tainted or not, killing the boy child might make his numerous other sons worry for their own fate and turn against him. For once, he paid attention. Fredric had six children by his now barren first wife, prior to the birth of the tainted one. Five hard fighting sons and a daughter he gave in marriage to the second most powerful man in his kingdom. Discomforting his greedy supporters, who thought one of them would have her.

To retaliate for the blow to his pride and the vow to keep Haven free from taint, Fredric personally saw to the extermination of his dead wife's family. Her father died by slow torture after Fredric made him watch the public execution of his four other adult children and their families. All were completely free of demon powers. The tainted child was given into the care of indifferent and fearful nurses in hopes of its demise. But against all odds Farrell survived to adulthood. He was kept in isolation, an object of ridicule and no little fear. His caregivers kept him blindfolded until he was old enough to keep his hypnotic gaze on the stones at his feet. When he had his first haircut, he raged and fought back for the first time, the pain beyond bearing. As punishment ever after, his hair was kept shorn to his scalp. So he grew delicate in body, startling at every shadow. Unbeknownst to anyone, powerful magical abilities were quelled by shock and ongoing terror.

\*\*\*

Lucan had ridden with an itch between his shoulder blades that could not be ignored ever since this mission began. The escort to take the boy to Daear was really quite inadequate for the brigand ridden trails through the forest and the battlefields. So many of Haven's soldiers still lay rotting in the sun. Scavengers, both human and coiled still roamed the destruction and Lucan feared their group would be attacked for the clothes they wore and their meager supplies. The country had fared worse than usual after another war effort. Frigid temperatures arrived early and the meager crops had been lost. The people were starving while the so called king harassed them for victuals to keep his soldier's tables heavy laden.

The day word spread that MeekBlade had fallen, hope had spurred a renewed effort on the part of the exhausted troops. They went out on the field the next morning expecting to beat the defenders back to the gates of the Citadel. The sight of a screaming virago on the back of a Pegasor, spearing warriors with a vengeance stunned everyone. She was flanked by the surviving complement of grim Cadre carrying the banner of their new Queen, who absolutely refused to leave the field until Fredric's army was in full retreat. The soldiers of Daear rallied under her banner and some said the Cadre chased the fleeing army into the pitch, slaughtering all they came upon. Lucan discounted those tales from terrified men. No one had chased him into that awful pitch as he attempted to assist any wounded back to safety. More often than not he could only put them out of their misery. Otherwise, their deaths would have been drawn out as they would receive little care and starved to death. From all he had heard the devotion of the Cadre to the ruler of Daear superseded any blood lust they might have for chasing wounded men in the pitch where a sensible man could expect ambush.

Lucan suspected with deserved paranoia why he had been called back to escort the boy into the enemy's realm. Surely they would both be killed by the mad woman the mountain people had put on their throne. Their arrival would be a mockery and an insult that would surely start another war effort. The slight figure in ragged clothes and llyncas frayed cloak had remained curled into a knot in the bottom of the wagon. Occasionally Lucan would ride close and look over the edge of the wagon side, but the knot would be drawn tighter, the head covered by crossed arms.

From what he had seen the boy had lead a miserable existence, appearing starved and frightened of every stir of breeze and jingle of harness. Lucan rode alongside for a while whispering urgent instructions and prayed the fearful bundle would react if it became necessary to flee on horseback.

Days later, the other men continued to avoid the prince with obvious loathing. Lucan dished up a bowl of traveler stew and pushed the food into the trembling hands with this foot. He was curious about the appearance of the boy, but the remembered trauma of that first day and rotations of rough treatment had reinforced the uncomfortable need to protect with nausea and fear sweat. He wondered if he could get past it to see the boy safely delivered. He could not eat anything and lay down on his bedroll, avoiding wrapping up in his blanket in case he needed his sword. At full pitch Lucan remained awake listening to every sound and the stirrings of the men lying around him.

They finally left the stench and horror of the killing fields taking the wagon road through the forest. What conversation there was dwindled away under the press of low hanging branches and deeply shadowed recesses where brigands could easily hide. Eventually the men surrounded the wagon, pulling together for mutual protection. Lucan slipped his sword free when the hair on the back of his neck stirred. The party traveled another mile before the gang of robbers attacked, yelling and brandishing their weapons. Lucan held his place beside the boy, hacking and clubbing anyone attempting to climb inside the open wagon. The other six men slashed and crushed skulls, but were hard pressed as the ragged gang was motivated by desperation. Two men were dragged from their saddles. Dead before the others could kill sufficient numbers to make the meager spoils not worth the continued effort of the wild eyed starving men.

Lucan refused to allow the others to give chase aware the brigands could easily take down a man in the thick undergrowth. This caused more grumbling and resentment that the upstart from the borders would think to command them. After all their commission was to see him dead along with the quivering rag in the wagon. Why wait until they were on Daear lands and then have to travel back through the forest again to get home?

By unspoken agreement the remaining four turned their mounts back to the wagon, telegraphing their ill intent. Lucan wasted no time reaching into the wagon and snatching the bag of bones from the wagon bed, flinging it across his saddle. He spun away, raced down the bend in the road, leaping the shallow ditch and plunging into the forest. Arrows embedded themselves into brush and trees at this back. He had not gone far before realizing the horse could not travel further though the dense foliage and tangled trees. Cursing under his breath, Lucan threw himself from the saddle, dragging the terrified prince with him. He dragged the body into the woods. The only remaining weapons were his sword and the blades he always secreted on his person. Somewhere behind him the abandoned horse whinnied. The sounds of the animal thrashing in agony could be heard along with the loud hissing of one of the larger forest predators who could not pass up such an opportunity. He hoped the noise covered his retreat into the undergrowth. Sometime later he went to ground beneath a huge old fallen pine, pushing the shuddering form into the loam of the forest floor. Now he had vicious beasts to fear as well as the foolish men who attacked him too soon to attain their goal. At least there were only a few desiccated Mathru husks tangled in the dead pine's branches.

The pursuers cursed and struggled in the woods, the ire of their King not to be trifled with if they returned without proof of the duo's demise. When the sounds of their frantic passage faded from the immediate vicinity, Lucan snatched his charge from the loam and dragged him further in the direction of the Citadel. He had no choice. There was no succor to be found anywhere except beyond the peaks of its gates. He moved swiftly, only going to ground again when the light completely faded, plunging the forest in an impenetrable pitch. Made more so by heavy rain clouds that obscured CatsEye and the scant stars. The next four days were a misery of continuous rain and chilly winds, heralding another early winter of desperation. At least the stench of the dead no longer plagued him.

\*\*\*

Pegasors did not like rain. They made their feelings about the weather clear to their riders with swiping fangs and a stubborn resistance to every command, until Talon lost his temper and clouted his stallion on its snarling mouth. The man growled as his grip on the reins twisted the muscled neck around and forced it into the mud. The tableau held for many long minutes. His threat to take a whip to the beast was met with flatten ears and hissing, but Talon would not relent one bit of pressure. He jerked the wide head up and forced the beast to look him in the eye. It was not long before the Pegasor's eyes rolled away. Talon was the dominant and it would not do for the stallion to forget it. The mares settled immediately and the troop continued on the muddy road, the stallion forging ahead growling all the while, his face plastered with muddy leaves.

The troop had been searching for two days on and off the forest road, hoping for some relief from the rain so the twins could pick up the scent of their quarry. Even now they scouted ahead, lost to sight except for their guardian and the escort, their task doubled as the twins quested all over for sign.

Nightfall once again found them all frustrated in their search. The Pegasors were sheltered beneath a stand of thick bramble firs and the troop made due with another cold camp. Wrapped in heavy blew throws, they shared smoked meat, journey bread and Mead from their medic's stores.

The Mead was not the honeyed drink of old earth, since

there was no such thing as honey on all of Nadredd. It was distilled from gwaed, toxic substances and venoms, by the hand of the one sitting on the throne. Many surmised it was some kind of narcotic or magic potion, addicting the Cadre and insuring their loyalty. In actual fact it inured them from most poisons. Fresh gwaed was deadly to humans and Gifted as well.

One of the first tests for a young squire was surviving their first taste of Mead without vomiting their stomach lining. There was a standing automatic death sentence for anyone even suspected of tampering with the brew. To be found in the wing housing the sovereign's laboratory was to be killed on the spot. It was placed directly into the hands of the Cadre medics and was forbidden for even a king to drink, that is before MeekBlade. It was the Cadres job to protect the sovereign or fall in the effort and the king's to provide the means, be it the purest metals from the southern FreeSoul domains and Mead. As MeekBlade and Bright Lance had been the first Cadres ever to sit on the throne the purity of the Mead was a certainty before ever being passed to the rank and file to consume.

Talisman checked each member for signs of illness due to the weather and made sure everyone ate a complete meal. The twins were settled on a portable cot in a tent. Although physically stronger than many so Gifted, no one took any chances with their well-being, to their amusement and expectation as their right. Talisman urged second helpings and cosseted everyone like a mother. He was teased about his obsessive worry over cold water. Were they not Cadre, the strongest of the strong? His face heated before their amusement, but their teasing finally caused him to settle and consume his own meal. Water beaded in the many ribboned braids on the medic's head, all gathered into a topknot. His dark burnished complexion marked him as a former member of the FreeSouls. He was the first of his people to ever depart for such a role in the demon's society. His family disowned him for the betrayal. A very few FreeSouls had surprisingly been Chosen, over the centuries, but no FreeSoul had ever entered Cadre service.

Talisman was nicknamed Romeo by his fellow Cadre for his devastating smile and its effect on the general female population. His dark brown eyes always sparkled with humor and affection. Women flocked around him. Lucky for them, Talisman had the heart of a baby in their regard. He was considered the good luck charm of the troop for his upbeat manner and his ability to sooth the hurt from minor wounds with his touch.

His people were descendants of ship's crew and colonists from Africa, the Far and Middle East, Island nations and the dissident Americas. They fled the military rule which dominated the first rotations as humans scrabbled for survival on Nadredd. These colonist were sick of the constant warfare of Earth and had hoped for a better life. The discovery of those first efforts implemented without their consent to affect their genetics caused many to flee government control once more. The military attempted to capture them in the beginning but eventually left them to be hunted by the Llyncu. The attacks tapered off as Llyncu died off in the wild.

Twenty five rotations later, the first generation of successful hybrids were being raised in Daear. FreeSouls were mining, living and surviving the harsh seemingly barren, mountain range to the south.

Now Healers and scientists of Stara freely exchanged knowledge with Daear. The Citadel did not claim them, but the relationship between their Senators and the throne was diplomatic even at its most frigid as the centuries passed.

Sticker settled next to Talisman, her big muscled body nudging him over until he almost toppled off the fallen log. He punched her in the shoulder and she beamed at him, enamored as most by his charisma.

Sticker was nearly as big as Talon. Had crushed the neck of enemies with her bare hands. Another of the most prized of the Queen's Cadre, her blond hair was already streaked with white and laugh lines marked her eyes and mouth. Sticker was another of jolly temperament and could find a joke in any circumstance, to the consternation of civilians expecting a woman to be less crude than men. She wore her ribbons of honor all the time The braided hair thick with red and black until it was a club of significant weight. In bar brawls Sticker had used that swinging bar of hair to strike the first blow, breaking more than a few jaws. Many of the Cadre shared her blew. It was no surprise to find more than one trooper sleeping curled next to her warm body in barracks or field. She reserved her favors for none. Loved each member of the Cadre with a single minded devotion that rivaled her loyalty to the ruler of their lands. She had no wish for the burden of command, but nurtured each new recruit through their first tough rotations.

Her blue eyes marked her as exotic in a land where even blondes were usually brown eyed. Refusing rank always insured the conniving courtiers had to lower their stuck up selves to find her favor, thinking big equaled dumb. Sticker was good at playing dumb. So it was many found their plotting undermined without ever connecting Sticker to their misfortune.

Sticker drank twice the rations in Mead and soup, nothing unusual for her. She dragged the protesting Talisman next to her body and slung her heavy arm around his shoulders, hugging him until he squeaked. Everyone around them grinned. Talisman, though not as tall as the woman beside him, was no little man. He wiggled in her grip until he planted a kiss on her cold lips and was dragged off into the dark to have his worry treated. He would be too exhausted to drive them crazy come dawn.

Some of the others settled together until their turn on guard. Two or three finding Sticker and Talisman beneath the trees. QuickStep spent part of the night with her teeth clenched on the cot struts while the twins assailed her body with coils, mouth and hands. The agonizing pleasure continued until she passed out. Talon heard her barely suppressed moans and ached for the touch of the Queen's hand. He turned his thoughts to the missing men and rejected the sleep his body demanded. The steady drip of rain on the fallen oak's leaves and bramble needles lulled most of the hard riding troop to sleep. However, each rotation of guards disturbed them all.

Dawn took them off the road once more only to return as the rain finally ended. They realized the entourage had not even arrived within their territory and sped along the muddy track. Five more dawnings found them once again camped without fire, the only sounds a few of the Pegasors feasting on a dearhart that roamed too near. Two dawns past, a chill wind began whipping through the trees and brought with it the odor of death. They were appalled that the opposing nation had not removed their soldiers for immolation. CatsEye would glow this night over acres of rotting corpses. Sometimes the enhanced senses of the crossbreeds could be a curse.

\*\*\*

Talon leapt from his bedroll, sword drawn, to find QuickStep racing into the trees behind the fleeing twins. The remaining forest creatures fled when an odd ululating wail split the silence.

"Four to me," Talon yelled and took off after them. Talisman and Fewfingers led the exodus, almost knocked aside as Raze and Brace sped passed them leaving the others to break camp and follow. Even if there were opponents about, the sound the twins were making would surely have them wetting their breeches by now. QuickStep had broken trail for them so they had little difficulty crashing through the underbrush in time to find the woman with her sword at the throat of an armored man with his own sword held en garde. He would not give ground even though the twins warbled and their hair entwined itself around the body of their Chosen. It did not take long to see he was frightened almost witless by the gold lit coiling strands. Peering into the dark, Talon managed to see a dark shape bundled at his feet.

"Hold QuickStep, Hold! Raze stand down!"

Both women lowered their swords on his order and Talon stepped forward.

"We are the Queen's Cadre. We seek news of King Fredric's son Prince Farrell, and the men riding with him."

The man's eyes watered and he shook with bitter laughter.

"I am the escort and your prince is here." He nudged the bundle of rags at his feet and the twins hissed in anger and their stilettos appeared.

"Pain and starvation Talon, pain!" The twins raged in unison and QuickStep immediately went to one knee and eased the quivering mass into her arms. There was only an anguished cry and Farrell went limp in her arms. It was no problem for the woman to bare the weight of what seemed to be a skeleton.

"The king's escort is hunting us. They cannot give up or he will kill them if they do not have proof of our demise. He has starved the boy and . . . "

"Enough", Talon waved him to silence. "We will take care of you both and return to the Citadel. It will be up to our Queen . . . "

"Talon, he is Gifted! They have kept his hair shorn Talon. How has he survived?" The Queen's Chosen grimaced at that pronouncement, remembering his own rotations of torturous pain under the clippers.

"QuickStep you and Talisman stay and care for him best you may. Strike, Shadow can you track them?" The twins heads went up and they spun about attempting to catch the wind driven scent.

"They are very near Talon. They hear you crash through

woods, hide now. Hide near. We go Talon, we go now?" Their bright golden eyes began to glow, even though their commander was immune to their hypnotic gaze, or so it seemed.

He considered the swaying twins, their unbound hair now lifted into the wind questing for the exact location of the enemy. The ultra-fine strands were highlighted by the deepening glow of their own eyes. The other man watched them in horrified fascination, never seeing their like before, only the tales told around the campfires and taverns. They truly were the embodiment of everything he was taught to fear.

"Go with stealth brothers, and take no chances. I would not lose you and QuickStep to these traitorous filth. Raze . . . "

Before he finished speaking they were all lost in the darkness. He saw QuickStep twitch in their direction, but held to her assignment. Talisman was already administering some type of inoculation and inserting an IV.

At that moment the remaining Cadre arrived, immediately setting up a new camp and pitching two tents. Talisman and QuickStep moved the young man into one, the medic requesting soup be heated and a cup of Pegasor blood be drawn right away. Brace and FewFingers guarded the perimeter of Prince Farrell's tent.

Sticker had been busy and the place for a good size campfire had already been prepared. Two of the men went among the trees and nicked the vein of one of the mares, drawing down the vitamin rich fluid that sustained Cadre in times of dire straits. Others quickly set up another tent a little ways out for the twins return. A successful hunt meant they would not tolerate anyone near their personal space for the remainder of the night. Everyone was busy and Lucan settled quickly by the fire his numb trembling hands held over the flames.

"Don't worry boy. We will have you both set to rights in no time."

The big woman gave him a wink and he watched her break open black bags and quickly mix dried meat, vegetables and noodles with water in a pot. Another man placed a metal grill over the lowering flames and hurried off to some other errand.

"Hurry boys, the poor soul needs blood while it is hot you know."

"On our way Sticker. Here you go Tal. Is he going to make it? Sure we can pitch the torches for you, no problem."

Men hurried from the tent and unpacked metal rods topped with a round globe from a bag, driving them into the ground at the entrance to the tent. One pulled a stick from the fire and quickly ignited the globes.

"There is oil trapped inside the ball. It burns until you smother it."

"I have never seen anything like that."

"It ain't magic boy, takes no conjuring to build a torch. We get some soup in you and set you right. You are a good bit. I might have something you can wear or Talon may."

Lucan looked to the tent where the dark haired commander stood, his eyes looking into the forest where he sent the odd twins to search. He could see the one called Tal and the younger blonde woman working over the prince, coaxing him to sip water. Then, with a bit more struggle, convince him to drink from the ceramic vessel filled with the blood of one of their strange Pegasors. He felt nauseous as he watched the boy finally taste, then finish the two disparate liquids. Tal came out again and searched through another canvas bag. He removed blankets and what could have been garments. The tent flap closed. After a little time Tal emerged with the prince's old clothes.

"Burn this stinking filth," he said to Sticker, "I would not shelter the worst of my enemies in such rags."

He cast a baleful glance in Lucan's direction and the blonde almost reached for his sword.

"How could you treat a Gifted One in such a way? Are you not the Chosen, what the coiling death were you thinking."

"Stand down Tal and return to your patient. He needs your attention more than you need to vent your ire."

The medic snorted and stomped off back to the tent. Talon sat down by the fire. His troop had encircled the camp, their ears tuned for the sounds of the twins successful hunt.

"Tell me your tale, that I will not find it necessary to cause that poor boy more pain by killing you."

Lucan stared into those opaque eyes and shuddered.

"I . . . do not understand what you mean. I am not a . . . a . . . chosen. I do not understand what you mean."

Talon stared back for a long time. Sticker passed tea to her charge and got up to find him some dry clothes.

"Talon can I look through your things for clothes?"

He seemed to consider for another interminable time and then nodded. Sticker searched around into another saddlebag. She returned to the fire with warm blew shirts and trousers in Cadre black. She sat down adding more vegetables to the pot.

"Stop sitting there shivering boy. Get out of those wet clothes now!"

Lucan jumped to his feet at the command tone before he realized it. He flushed in embarrassment. Then his move away from the fire was countered by the sudden appearance of Talon's sword.

"Until we leave this forest remain ever at my side. Tell me again why you should continue to live."

Lucan knew such frustration he began to yell.

"I do not know what you mean. I keep saying that! I was sent away to become a killer for the king instead of the gardener like my father all because I found that boy in the kitchen garden! They beat him. They beat me for touching him and dragged him away. But I did not die in the fights against your kind. He did not die though it appears they did all they could to make it happen! I do not understand what you expect me to do. What could I do against men with swords when I had never touched a sword in my life! I can not help you. I can not touch him. I . . . I . . . "

He turned away and staggered into the bush to fall to the ground stricken with vomiting, losing what little tea he had managed to ingest.

Talon picked up the fallen clothes and stood over the stricken man. He waited until his illness abated.

"You and the prince have been wronged beyond bearing and I do not know if the breach can be healed. To the Citadel you will go and we will see what my Queen and the Gifted at court have to say. Ease off, I will not burden you again. Put on the clothes and try to rest, we move out at first light."

Shaking and unable to articulate the latent pain that had flared to agonizing life within his center, Lucan clutched the clothes to his chest and struggled into them. Talon walked away from the shaken soldier and went to the tent to check on his new charge. Suddenly a wail went up in the dark forest. The Pegasors answered it with roars and hisses. The ululation frightened Lucan white. QuickStep rushed from the tent and took off into the forest, making a loud wailing imitation of the sound. A   prolonged agonized screaming from one of the wretches that wanted to kill him added a horrible accompaniment.

Four of the guards returned to the fire and got cups of now simmering soup and drank some black arcane liquid poured by the big woman at the fire. Tal emerged from the tent and admonished her.

"Sticker do not pour too much. I swear you think Mead is nothing but beer for you to ingest for pleasure. Stay your hand from the medkit or I will report you to the BareBlade."

The woman snorted.

"Report me and your nights will be a lot colder Tal-is-man." She snagged him around the waist and tumbled him into her lap, kissing him soundly, to the delight of the other men gathered.

The cries rising from the forest drew closer and the threesome breezed into camp. The twins hair reached Talon first, twining about this face and threading through his hair. Contact was made with the finer strands that those outside the Cadre were unaware he had. The wavering strands caressed and withdrew. The twins dragged QuickStep away to further initiate her into new pleasures of oneness with a Gifted. A moment later Raze appeared in the firelight her armor obscured from the blood of one who would kill no longer. Her teeth were bared in a macabre grin heightened by the smears on her face, as she showed the commander her bloodied short blade. Talon face was grim as he acknowledged her kill before returning to the fire. Raze disappeared again into the trees to clean the blood from her body and armor.

"Fredric's killers are no more. They suffered for their plans to torture him to death. Understand this Lucan of Haven, the joining of Llyncu and human is respected in Daear. The Gifted are highly prized and in the past men have fought over the right to join their families to a Gifted line. Our Queen's mother was from such a family and although weak in body her powers of mind were a great boon to our people. The poor spies your king sent just after our MeekBlade sat on the throne were apprehended because she dreamed of their entrance into our lands. Together Caron and MeekBlade ruled our people with wisdom and we prospered. We will continue, as a joined people, for as long as CatsEye commands the sky. And BrightLance will rule until her true death if I must put down who ever or whatever stands in her way."

Lucan swore and drew away from the bright fire that flashed when Talon heavy lashes lifted from silver orbs.

"Enough intimidation, leave the boy be Talon."

Sticker shoved her Captain aside and wrapped the trembling blonde in a heavy blew cloak and dragged him closer to the fire, settling him on the ground beside her. Before

Talon could say anything else, she pressed a cup of soup into Lucan's hands and made him sip. Her muscled arm wrapped snug around his shoulders. Talon sighed heavily. The man had been though much and he was not being fair. It was obvious Lucan had been kept in ignorance and abused most of his life. A gardener's son, who can imagine one with such a spirit forced to kill. In Daear, those of gentle spirit nurtured the land and fauna or healed the sick. They were defended with much zeal as the survival of all depended on their abilities to wrest sustenance from the dangerous world. Lucan knelt at the fireside and faced the downcast man.

"I beg pardon Chosen of Farrell. I have been rude to one sorely tried. I ask forgiveness." He lowered his head waiting for the judgment. Lucan gaped at him, not quite understanding that the formidable warrior was apologizing. Sticker hugged him against her side and said.

"The ornery Pegasor is asking forgiveness, boy. Say accepted or call him out and settle it with swords!"

"What, are you all mad? Is everyone around me insane? Enough, enough I'm so tired of killing!" His rising voice edged into hysteria. Sticker plucked him off the ground and cradled him, murmuring and crooning as he struggled until exhaustion finally won out. He lay boneless staring up into the woman's face that rocked like his own mother long ago. She had died all alone and starving after his father had died on a battlefield, conscripted into service by the fool who claimed a non-existent throne.

Tears came at the thought and Sticker cuddled him to her armored breast. He was destined to spend the night cradled in her protective arms and in the following weeks, she would become his ever present protector. Talisman dug around in his kit and came up with a hypodermic and injected a sedative so Lucan would rest through the night. He had been strained beyond bearing for many rotations and had reached the end of his ability to cope.

"He needs respite from the fighting Talon and a chance to recover from all he has suffered. His mind might not survive much more." The medic helped Sticker snug him in more blankets and they both settled him against her side to rest. Fewfingers stirred the soup pot and dished up bowls that he carried to the guards and made sure the twins and QuickStep had their share, which he left at the entrance to their tent. He ignored the whimpers and moans and hurried away. The twins were at their most dangerous and territorial after a hunt. They had been known to lash out at Cadre members before their guardian had arrived to sooth the aggression and fear that rode them. No one wanted to irritate them into thinking the Chosen was threatened.

Fewfingers settled down to his own meal, smirking as Talisman wiggled down in the blankets along Sticker's other side. He wondered if the silly man was jealous. Fat lot of good it would do him. Sticker was big on comfort, thank the forbearers'. Nearly all of the Cadre had benefited from the pleasure and safety her body afforded them. He reached and lifted the cup of Mead, drinking it down in two quick swallows. He watched his glum Captain staring into the flames, feeling bad about scaring the boy worse than he already was.

"Come Chosen, you should sleep. You have not rested these many days."

"He is correct Talon. You are no good to us if you are not rested to protect these two," Talisman interjected from the depth of his blankets.

"Fine I will sleep, but . . . "

"Never you mind. Farrell will not awaken before the sun is high. Both of them need the rest."

Sighing, which made Fewfingers grin, the Queen's Own snatched up his blew and settled grumpily by the fire. One more sigh escaped before he gave up the struggle to remain awake. The grey haired officer gathered his blew and settled down against his Captain's back. He wrapped his right arm over the big man's waist and snugged him into his body, his leather wrapped scarred hand holding Talon close.   The sleeping man sighed again and rolled over onto Fewfingers's chest.

Talon was fanatical about his duty and it took a lot to get him down to rest. Brace and TauntBow, crawled over and settled around him, knowing sometime in the night Talon would be wrapped around them all, finding comfort in the pile he had denied himself for too many days. He was a loner compared to the others in the troop. Only taking comfort in the field and then only when wounded or exhausted.

Brace was fairly new to the troop, but had developed a case of hero worship that survived the passing rotations. Brace had not hesitated to plant himself at Talon's back during his first skirmish and beat back every man which attempted to strike down the Queen's Own. It had become his permanent place and name. Strands of his light brown hair eased from its braid to twine with Talon's during the dark. He had been shocked to hear that Talon spent his youth with his hair shorn. No child with coils, powers or no, was required to cut their hair as youth in training. It was a horrible distraction of constant pain. That fact made Talon nearly invincible to Brace's eyes.

The light of dawn rose behind murky clouds and drizzle. Giving the exhausted troop the excuse to burrow deeper into their blankets and share a few extra hours of body heat. Talisman was as reluctant as anyone else to leave Sticker's blankets, but his patients needed tending. The prince slept restlessly, disturbed by nightmares and the ongoing pain of his shorn head. Lucan slept like a stone and Talisman knew someone would have to carry both their charges. Riding was out of the question. He checked his stores and grimaced over the depletion of Mead. He rationed the remaining powder into packets concealed beneath his armor, leaving only enough for each warrior to have one cup. Sticker would just have to cope, or there would not be enough to see them home. She would be contrite, but it would still be gone. She was irritating beyond bearing sometimes, but he loved her like no other woman.

Cadre did not marry, but mated among themselves until death broke the pairing or the lovers drifted into the arms of another. They were too suspicious of motivations to trust outsiders with their sovereign's life. Children were not an option. They could be hostages. Many men and women of the Cadre were sterilized on acceptance into the troop if they had civilian family members to carry on the family bloodlines.

Talisman reminded himself to check TauntBow over before riding out. The bowman's brown eyes were a little bleary and Tal knew for all his bluster a cold was coming on.

TauntBow was a very even tempered man until he caught a cold, then he whined like a child. The medic worried that TauntBow's susceptibility could mean more serious problems in his later winter rotations. He mixed a tea that the warrior would drink if Tal had to get Sticker to sit on him.

Talisman's grandfather had seen the archives and told his medics in training that no cure existed for the irritating disease. People were rarely ill due to cancers or neurological diseases, almost always falling prey to the flora or fauna of Nadredd. Death following swiftly if a Healer was not practically in their back pocket. Finally satisfied with his preparations for the dawn, the medic went to stir up the fire, boil the water for tea and warm the Mead. He would be heartily sick of soup by the time he got home.

The dark guard came in and began packing up the camp. The sleeping troop rolled out, tended their dawning abulations and drank down the ration. Some exchanged places with the dark guards. The others fed dried meat to their mounts and loaded the packs before saddling up. The relieved men ate dried fruit and bread to break their fast. Everyone else would eat as they rode.

Talon tended his stallion, the troop scattering to give him space as the snarling, fang gnashing beast reminded them why Pegasors were feared. In the end his heaving and clawing availed him nothing. He stood trembling with ire as the Commander saddled him. Finally they moved out, Lucan snug and still asleep in the arms of Sticker. The prince in a hammock rocking gently between the twin's Pegasors. He was hooked to more than one IV and the sedative kept him oblivious. Talon occasionally rode back from the head of the column to gaze at the youth. Appalled at his condition, Talon wondered how his Queen's ire would be expressed. Fredric hoped to murder the boy and blame Drear. Would they go to war over this? Talon's heavy sigh did not go unnoticed by the twins. Their thought reflected his own, except where he was weary, they were anticipating, predator's to their very souls.

QuickStep's mount circled the twins and their charge, her eyes continuously scanning the forest for danger. Her body was sated almost more than she could stand. Really she would rather be sleeping. But her Gifted were focused on easing the young man's pain and not their surroundings. She would rather die than allow them to come to harm. Her heart swelled with love immediately drawing the attention of the twins. She gave them an embarrassed smile and rode on. Their hair gently caressed the boy's stubble, communicating comfort and pleasure, sensations never before experienced and rather frightening even in his unconscious state. Farrell realized he was helpless. Once more his fate was in the hands of more powerful beings. He did not care any longer.

When the rain began to fall again, the twins covered the prince with another blanket and propped him higher in the sling so he would not think he was drowning. Talon did not wish to stop right away. His anxiousness to get back to Daear, communicated itself to beast and troop. They all wanted to camp away from the stench and the threat of Fredric sending troops when his men did not return.

It was very late into the second dawn, before the troop made camp again. They moved with their usual efficiency. Once the prince and his protector were settled into the tent, everyone gathered around the fire. The twins had made a dash into the woods and returned with a dearhart, which was dressed very quickly and now roasted over the fire. Talon gave the liver and heart to his stallion. Brace sat at his back allowing the exhausted commander to rest against him. Talon had spent as much time on the back trail as the others, making sure they weren't being tracked. They dared not assume there were no more men in the field. Sticker sliced the meat onto the platters for each man and they ate with relish. The twins soaked up the appreciation of the troop for the change in diet.

Their questing hair darted around caressing hair and faces, the contact more exact communication than mere words for them. The racial memory of killing humans was ever present, but the ancestry passed down by their parents, had prevented anything more than temper tantrums in the past. Now that they had QuickStep, the predator was soothed even more. Possession of a Chosen was the nearest thing to fulfilling the urge to consume. They tortured their protector, true enough, but with unbearable pleasure. It was fulfilling in a way they could have never explained. It was consuming but not.

The overall atmosphere of the campers lightened the closer they drew to the ragged peaks of home. The remainder of the journey passed without incident. Talisman kept the prince and Lucan sedated the entire way. Talon sent Raze ahead to warn the Queen. This would not be a welcoming with feast and music, but a desperate bid to heal mind, bodies and a fractured bond. The first two possible, the latter would be a miracle.

Raze was smallest in stature among the Cadre, but she made up for it with a viciousness that never found release except in battle. Her sword arms was heavily muscled and she was even handed. Her head was shorn except for the thick black braid she wore chignon. She wore it thus and used one of her own lethal small blades to keep her pate devoid of any hair. No one knew how much pain she may feel, if any. There had never been sign of gifts in all the rotations she rode for the Cadre. She loved close work and her opponents died cut to ribbons or hacked in two. The last thing they saw was the pitiless black orbs of their killer and her scarred visage. She was as Talon, sharing her blankets with no one except in the field. In her case, only when someone was fatally wounded, which was rarer still, as Cadre fought to the death more often than not.

Speculation spread like wildfire though the palace as the checkpoints reported Raze rushing through reserving her report for the Queen alone.

When the troop arrived at the first security checkpoint, they were relieved to see additional guards were on duty and all the torches along the summit ablaze. They wasted no time in conversation other than to warn the men to be wary of spies daring this close because the young prince had not been killed but rescued. Talisman's raced away to see that the preparations made to care for the prince and his damaged protector were in place to his satisfaction. He would also make sure the squires were on hand to assist the tired troop settling in for the night. Before his own head rested on a pillow the Healer will have run himself ragged in his concern for everyone's well-being.

Talon rode at the head of the troop when they arrived on the terrace. The Queen stepped out immediately to hear the news. Talon wanted to admonish her for remaining awake so late in the night, but he was really too tired and she was no longer a child. She flung herself across the parquet into his arms. He hugged her close and assured her all the troop were returning unscathed. She held his wrist in one small hand as he escorted her to the twins who had dismounted to check on the little prince. They rolled the blankets back so the Queen could look upon her future husband. She had been told, but it was not the same as seeing for herself. A hiss escaped her lips and muscles locked. Her anger swept like a wave over the troop. Some placed hands on their weapons in response. The twins hissed back and their hair lifted searching for prey. She shivered and spoke softly to the agitated hunters. BrightLance began to hum a wordless tune that settled everyone much to their collective surprise. Talisman hurried through the gate directing Caregivers and troops laden with care baskets to place the prince and the befuddled Lucan into for transport. They were headed for quarters in the Queens tower of the palace. He assured Talon that a fresh posting of guards had just come on duty to see to the Queen's protection and watch over the patients and the doctors the Queen had assigned to treat them.

"You will not spend the night standing before my door protecting me from men too ill to walk let along attempt to attack me. I have complete trust in all the Cadre. I will rest well as will all of you in your beds!"

She reiterated her statement with a stern eye at Talon and the twins.

"If the prince has any problems the Healers cannot handle I will certainly send someone to bring Strike and Shadow to assist. All of you have done well to save two lives. It is time you took your rest. Don't make me order you to do what is common sense."

Talon's felt admonished, which he was. He managed to maintain his dignity, so the blush did not manifest on his face.

"As you will it my Queen."

Bright Lance smiled at the exasperated Chosen. Small fingers caressed his cheek and sent reassurance and pride to her ever vigilant protector. She felt his worry fade and tense muscles relaxed even further under her hand, as it should be.

"We will speak of events tomorrow four bells before last meal. Reports should be available by then from the Healers as well. For now rest well and I do mean just that."

BrightLance gifted them with one of her dazzling smiles, spun away to catch up to the retreating Cadre and their charges. Her voice floated back to them taking Talisman to task for not heading off to bed. They listened to her cajoling until her voice faded from the most attentive ears.

Shaking off the minor enthrallment, the troop gave up their tired mounts to squires rushing onto the terrace with StraightBow keeping a wary eye from the shadows. Talon's troop left them to it, walking with weary steps into the palace proper and headed in mass along the wide corridor to their barracks. Behind them the squires hustled the deceptively docile Pegasors onto the freight elevators that would drop them off at the terraced corral and barn four floors below.

The stone floor and walls gradually gave way to gleaming metal in a straight on hallway. It lead to access hatches to the sovereign's apartments and the palace proper. Four of the Cadre were on guard duty in the surrounding dark unseen to the untrained eye. The returning troops made a sharp right turn here and at the end of a short corridor walked down a ramp that formed a very tight spiraled walkway down. There were no scones in the walls for lighting. The Cadre traversed the ramp in total darkness regardless the time of dawn or dark. It was a well-known saying among the people that if a Cadre member did not express extreme paranoia at all times, they were surely an imposter. No assassin had yet to penetrate the Palace and certainly not the Cadre's personal quarters.

The rooms were carved out of the mountain below the sovereign's apartments. Wide portals hallowed out of the mountainside opened onto the green vistas of Daear's terraced city and its gardens. The wide valley contained the city's other institutions and the community grids, where much of the farming and animal husbandry was conducted alongside homes, shops and taverns. Cavernous greenhouses were filled with enhanced vitals that the people still did not allow the soil of Daear to nurture. Barns with reinforced flooring housed the enhanced horses of the Diligence Calvary alongside other outbuildings for the cattle, the domesticated dearharts experiment and muskies. Beyond the city could be seen smaller self-contained communities and the keeps of the Barons. It was a colorful scene in a drab world.

After days of hunting in enemy territory, more than one of the troop paused to look out on the haven they fought so hard to maintain. Talon' eyes were refreshed by the sight and he lingered until Brace pulled him away to seek the comforts of the steam baths and bed. Besides the barracks and hygiene facilities, there were the offices of the General and Captains; meeting rooms, training facilities and the medic center. After much needed sleep everyone would be debriefed before going to report to the Queen and hear what updates may be had on the refugees health.

\*\*\*

Baron Vidor entered the conference hall, his gaze over the expansive room noting the fireplaces that encircled the room all alight. The oil globes flame cast further light to combat the chilling effect of grey metal. He was grateful for it as the days had turned quite cold and the partial metal walls seemed to radiate the cold in his direction. Bright colorful holographic pictures of stars, Origin Earth, and galaxies were placed above the mantels of each fireplace, adding another impression of warmth to the room. His old bones appreciated the warmth so he shook the heavy burgundy, woolen cloak from broad shoulders and handed it off to the cadet to put it away. He smoothed the grey sweater, knitted in a long tunic style down over burgundy wool slacks and was very thankful for the 'long johns' beneath them. The fact no one but the Cadre was permitted to wear weapons in the Queen's presence relieved him of heavy sword and scabbard. The attendant graced him with a sweet smile and introduced herself as Mila, before returning to her duties. Cadets in the Queen's compartments wore a variation of the ancient ship's crew uniform, black woolen shirt and pants with the hems tucked into calf length flat heeled boots. An imaginative image of the Milky Way galaxy was embroidered near their left shoulder. The symbol had been favored by King MeekBlade and his daughter did not appear to want it change it. Besides, the cadets attire brought to mind the Cadre and Vidor feared the brooding color would become a new fashion at court. He was not a flamboyant dresser by any means, but everyone running around in black would be very depressing he thought.

The Baron's expression darkened, considering their King had fallen in battle and put his untried daughter on the throne. Then again, perhaps that description was no longer apt because discounting their field units were outnumbered, at least in bodies, Daear had once again emerged victorious. The 'little girl' leading her Cadre to break the enemy front line and killing everyone who came within reach of her spear stunned more than the enemy. She struck true and often to the horror of the Barons and foot soldiers.

Stirred by her vicious cursing of the enemy, the Diligence Calvary rushed in to reinforced the Cadre assault by breaking the right flank of the enemy. They were led by Baron Colwyn and his brothers Gavin and Nardo. Drunkard he might be but not many shared the sheer ferocity of Nardo. Why he had not been killed was a mystery to many for he fought with no regard for caution, usually drunk off his head.

They left Renfrew to the left flank, but were surprised when half his company, led by his sons appeared in the midst of the enemy like a geyser erupting. The screams of Fredric's soldiers jellied the bowels of their fellows as blood rained down upon the unscathed and sent them running in confusion. The wily baron struck. The panicked soldiers were crushed between him and his exultant sons, their coils snapping necks and sword flashing in the sunlight as they laughed.

Baron Renfrew was Gifted and although his wife was one of Vidor's own non gifted granddaughters, he bred true. The three boys she bore were powerful. They appeared bred for war and nothing pleased the young ones more than to follow their father onto the field. The Baron was proud of the covert forays his sons had successfully completed for King MeekBlade and his predecessor. No one was sure how it was done. Renfrew's own gift eluded everyone and he distracted the curious with haughty demeanor, flirting, and an insane smile.

Two of the hellions had already sired children, while the heir continued to entertain many but marry none. Out of all of the Barons, Renfrew was the most secure Gifted, politically. He was favored by the populace because he brought their fantasies of romantic love between Llyncu and human to life and was a generous employer. The nobility had hoped the Gifted one would take other wives, spreading his genes more, but he favored his 'pure' wife. It was not custom to limit one's self to a single wife or husband when alliances were the currency that kept the government afloat. The old man believed his granddaughter was Chosen even if it went unacknowledged. Whichever, love or Chosen, Vidor was grateful for her sake as she was doted on, protected fiercely and now was caring for the middle son Rhys' triplets. Once again the negotiators were anxious hoping at least this second son would remarry. However since the death of his wife in childbirth, Rhys entertained no one, focusing his attention on leaving carnage in his wake on the battlefield.

With a relieved sigh Vidor sat down at the metal table, resting against the back of the metal seat. These furnishings were said to be part of the original ship that housed the now Queen's apartments. He thought it was so because the floor beneath their feet was metal deck plating and the table and chairs were bolted in place. Vidor noted two of the chairs at the table were draped in the bloodied estate flags of Baron Kane and his half-brother Baronet Glasius. Their betrayal had cost the people dearly and pushed Daear into this unwanted war. Vidor remained exhausted from the fighting. Honestly he was too old to be slogging on foot and fighting hand to hand. But Baron Caddock, for all his ability in a fight, had no head for strategy and Meinrads' surly attitude made for obstinance at the worst possible times. The foot soldier's commanders had taken the brunt of it, so someone had to step in. Although still slim as in his youth, the iron grey hair and lines around deep brown eyes only hinted at his true age. StraightBow was his younger brother and they both had seen many Kings take the throne.

Although considered 'pure' human, Vidor had been able to make advantageous marriages, out living even his Gifted wives. His keep teemed with his descendants and successful marriages had been made within the FreeSouls Alliance, the wandering Searchers and a few of the lessor 'nobility'. His get married for love, and it had paid off in support for Daear bolstered by sometimes tenuous familial connections since a few of his grandchildren had married even further afield into the Rovers and Coastal Dwellers.

After such a decisive victory and the successful rescue of young Prince Farrell, the old man hoped that Fredric's pursuit of eliminating Daear's supposed threat would come to an end. The Daear were tired of the constant state of warfare since Fredric ruled in Haven. At least most of them were. He discounted Renfrew and his own great grandsons from that equation with a rueful smile lighting his face.

Mila appeared at his shoulder, begging his pardon as she placed a flagon of steamed cider before him. He thanked her profusely until she blushed before taking a grateful sip from the hot, mildly alcoholic beverage that warmed him to the core. He watched her place full pitchers over the hot plates in the table to keep the beverage steaming. She hurried away and returned with platters of fragrant meat pies and warmed damp towels which she placed in a recess of the table to keep them moist. Once the Queen arrived no cadets would be allowed in the conference room until she retired.

He didn't bother turning to see the next personage enter the room. Caddock gave the girl a loud hearty greeting and made his way to the table. He gave the usual grunt, in greeting Vidor, poured some cider and settled at the middle of the table.

"The wind is like knives today. I would rather be still in my blankets than sitting in all these damn meetings."

"I drank to that. My bones are too old for fighting all day, traveling day and night, and trying to placate my madhouse family."

"There is that."

Caddock laughed and scratched at his windblown hair. Even his heavy brown beard was ruffled. It took more than a few tugs and twists to straighten the woolen navy blue tunic he wore with black slacks and scuffed black boots threaded with leather strings. Vidor thought it would have been an easier process if he would just remove the empty scabbard from his waist, but he did not say anything, just smiled. Sometimes Caddock was as scatter brained as a child.

"There are times I do not envy you old man. You have

an army all yelling at once for your attention and some of them are still in nappies!"

The two men laughed together. There was no doubt about it. It took brandishing his sword and swearing, to get control of the rabble that descended on the palace the day after word went out the fighters had returned. He sent his children and grands that were designated to confirm his survival packing off home with a few good swats on the ass to boot! They were old enough to know better.

"It was good to rest eyes upon them, but they were never a quiet lot. I thought the headache would kill me and the coddling! Rosyn actually wanted to sit by my bed and fluff my pillows all night. I could not get her out of here with the rest of them. She insists on taking care of me as if my wits went with my last winter celebration. I left her scalding the hide off our cook for serving my steak too rare."

Vidor could not help but smile though. His Rosyn truly took good care of her grandfather. If only some young man had come along and captured her fancy. Between her constant attention to his every waking moment, her midwifery and herding the multitude of children that occupied the estate, Rosyn insisted she did not have time to entertain any husbands, Gifted or otherwise. Vidor had finally quit pestering her, resigned to being harassed to the end of his days.

Baron Caddock found it all very amusing. His get were all at his estate with his heir Brice running things while he rode off to war. He had not been able to bear risking any of his precious sons. Although they were trained to fight he forbade them unless he fell.

They were still laughing, trading stories about their

families, when the door was opened again.

A harried looking young man rushed into the room burdened with a flimsy box and stylus to take a seat across from Caddock. Baronet Celyn was just nineteen. He had not gone to the front lines, but his face was already lined with care and grief.

"How are you faring lad? Are your mother and brother's wife recovering?", Caddock inquired.

"Thank you for your concern sir. Mother was prepared strangely enough. She says she knew Stone and Taffye would not return this time just as she knew father would not return. When word came, her tears were already dry. Taking care of Marietta is her focus now. It is near her time but, but mother does not think she will survive long after the baby comes."

Baron Vidor reached across the table and grasped the slim shoulder in commiseration.

"I will speak to my Rosyn, she can travel with you and assist your mother if she will have her."

"Yes lad, if you need assistance you only have to say and mine will do whatever we can. These are the times when we all must support each other. No need to face your struggles alone. We are all willing and are able to assist." Caddock reached across the table a gave the young man's wrist a firm grip as well.

Celyn attempted to contain his emotions, but could only nod and fight back his tears. Baron Vidor poured another flagon of cider and bid the young man to drink.

"Give yourself time to breath son. I know it seems like the world is climbing on your shoulders now, but we will help. Take your time."

The older men left him to himself for a while to settle and contemplated their own good fortune. They ignored his quick swipe at watering eyes, leaving the sleeve of his russet tunic damp and his blue/grey eyes red rimmed. He busied himself organizing paperwork from the small brown satchel he had carried in over his shoulder. While he waited for the meeting to begin, he might as well address some of his family's estate matters. If he wrote down what he intended to do perhaps he would not miss anything and regret it later. There was just so much.

Baroness Tesni and Branwen entered the room together, chatting and snickering like two young girls paying no attention to the men around the table. Branwen's waist length auburn tresses were entwined with Tesni's short curly brown hair even though the little Baroness was head blind to any magic whatsoever. Only after giving into complete hilarity did the two women wipe their eyes and, still snorting, make their way to the table.

The older men could not help but watch in fascination as Branwen's coils slipped free of her friends hair. Perhaps the illusion of communication was comforting to the Gifted one.

"Forgive our manners gentlemen. Branwen just received the most ludicrous marriage proposal. I . . . "

Tesni gave way to laughter again. Her cheeks were quite rosy and brown eyes were alight with humor. She remembered that her cloak was still around her shoulders and apologized to the young lady waiting patiently to put it away. She gave her arms a brisk rubbing to discard the chill her pine green woolen gown did not quite prevent. She had only returned to the palace in time for the meeting and met Branwen along the way.

"Why would that officious little excuse for a man think I would want to give up my independence to listen to him moan and whine about the injustices of his lot?"

Baroness Branwen settled into the chair next to Vidor, reaching over and giving Celyn's arm a squeeze. Her best friend Tesni was still caught up in laughter and just managed to fall into the chair between Vidor and Caddock.

"Well it wasn't actually a marriage proposal. It was more of an invitation to contract."

Tesni was once again laughing her head off.

"Oh my," she gasped, "it was not the proposal that set me off. It was the look on your face."

Branwen glared at her best friend, but could not hold it and dissolved into laughter again.

"I expect he will not be so forward in the future. I am very pleased with my life as it is. I certainly do not have time to be pregnant and fulfill my duties, especially in the current situation."

Baroness Branwen's comment brought the hilarity to an momentary end reminding everyone about the reasons for this new meeting of the leaders of their people. Because she had very powerful telekinesis, Branwen taught at the University to help others hone their ability. Her classes were only one week a term because she had to see to running her estate and staying in contact with her children, who also needed her training. She did not find spending time at court odious as gifted were very social by design.

Her second husband had given her a great responsibility and Vidor and Caddock was enough old fashioned to think it was ill done of him to run off with the Searchers and explore while leaving Branwen to raise his heir, run the estate and keep up the political affiliations necessary to hold the barony. Never the less they also could not discount the fact that Branwen was thriving on the challenge.      Right    at    this moment Branwen looked refreshed and ready for what came. Her cheeks were flushed and that one bright topaz eye sparkling, overshadowing the brown one. She was exceptionally slim and lacked height as did Tesni, although she had an inch or two over her friend. At first impression many believed her no more than a child. Then she would open her mouth and they would be dissuaded. She wore a dull brown woolen gown and boots, which Caddock thought did nothing for her looks at all. Branwen would be considered plain of face by anyone, but the sheer power she processed made her a popular target of the alliance negotiators for marriage or contract. As far as she was concerned her part had been done with three husbands and a child for each.

Caddock was on the mark and served the ladies a flagon each of cider. After a few sips the question of who had offered Branwen a contract returned. It was certainly not done to accost any woman in public about such matters. If a family had not the money for a negotiator, then the most senior member of the house approached the senior of the house in question. Considering Branwen's status, she could be hostile enough to demand recompense for the embarrassment. Whoever this idiot was, he had been saved by sheer luck. Even Branwen's current husband in residence could take up retaliation if she wished it. Although both of the old men could not imagine First Accountant Toru taking up arms.

Branwen immediately starting laughing again. She loved Toru very much, but surely he would talk the miscreant to death before raising a sword!

"I will tell him over dinner tonight. If he is offended I will remind him the annoyance is already embarrassed in front of Tesni."

"And just what do you mean by that? I am no gossip Brainy!"

Once again the men were laughing at the glare 'Brainy' shot across the table.

"Do not insist on using that accursed name you brat. Beside how else will I get my revenge if you do not whisper in someone's ear so it will be all over the court before first meal?"

"Oh. Well when you put it that way." A big grin of pure devilment lit up Tesni's face.

"It is a deal. Just remember you owe me a favor now." Brown curls bounced around her face as she nodded her head vigorously causing her friend to roll her eyes.

"Yes, yes favor acknowledged."

"So are you two going to tell us who it was? The suspense you know." Caddock attempted to give them a pleading look, which everyone found humorous.

"Would you believe that odious Quartermaster was lurking in the hallway when I came out of the refresher near the old ship galley? I thought I was being smart to get in there for an early breakfast, especially since the palace guards are the only ones that use it. If Tesni hadn't appeared I might not have been able to avoid putting him through a wall. Imagine trying to have babies just to advance you status? I do not think he has even seen any of his children since they were born!"

Branwen's statement had raised her ire once more and her hair lifted and wafted around her shoulders. She shook herself and the locks settled gently on the shoulders of the oblivious Celyn and Vidor's arm, massaging gently. No one missed the boy relaxing back against his chair as the lady's coils slipped into his own auburn hair. But he continued to scribble away, intent on his flimsy.

"Folant has long since lost all propriety in his quest for a higher station. In the past his family has always been proud of their duty to the Ship and the Captains. I know for a fact he has lost the one child he was counting on to barter for marriage. Young Kayin has been accepted into Cadre training."

Vidor volunteered that bit of gossip with a rueful expression on his face. It was not his want to gossip at any time, except about his prolific family of course.

"No reason to be shamed Vidor. It is common knowledge that the latest squire is exceptionally talented and can communicate with the Pegasors and the Diligence Calvary mounts. I have already asked the Commander to allow the boy time off for extensive gene mapping. There have been very few beast communicators over the centuries. We would be foolish to ignore this opportunity to discover what family lines came together to create this affect. Veterinarians in Animal Husbandry are also requesting time with the young man to see if he can obtain information that could give some insight into the more difficult afflictions that plague our cattle, particularly those huge ox beast the Rovers use."

Baroness Tesni ceased speaking before she got carried away. She was a geneticist, as had her family members been through the centuries. The great reveal had appalled her as it had many of her fellows, but attempting to reverse what is, would hasten the demise of civilization as they knew it. She worked tirelessly for better health and viability of offspring, rather than attempting to go back to before the ships touched down on Nadredd.

"Well if it makes those beast the Cadre ride more tractable I say let him pass with flying colors. It is a shame that even allies have to avoid injury when they are around", Caddock grumbled. It was well known he hated the Pegasors, since one took a bite out of him during a moment of devilment in his youth. Vidor hid his grin behind his hand and then refilled everyone's flagon.

There was tumble of voices at the entrance and the group turned as one to welcome the newcomers.

Baron Renfrew and his heir Haul bustled through the door, nodded to Mila and rushed the table. They wore sleeveless tunics of pale green with black slacks and boots. Renfrew's boys were as immune to the cold as their father was. It was unusual to see any of them in heavy clothing unless it was complete battle armor. Renfrew sketched a bow at the company with the usual crazy grin on his face. His topaz eyes were bright with a maniacal glint. Haul matched his father's grin and flung his arms around great grandfather Vidor, giving him a squeeze.

"You look well GG. I am starving. Do we have food yet?" Haul laughed as his great grand squirmed in his hold. The seasoned warrior took great joy in needling Vidor, and his long unbound hair wrapped around the old man's shoulders and slipped into his hair. His voice dropped to a whisper as he continued to hug him.

"Your injuries are healing well sir?"

"Not to worry yourself you little heathen. I was barely in bed a day before I had to chase the herd out of the castle." Vidor reached up and buried one hand in Haul's pale strawberry blonde hair, scratching his scalp and laughing more when the man began to purr in his ear.

"Arr! Stop doing that you sneaky old devil." Haul pulled away his face going crimson.

"First rule of tactics. If it is not broken do not repair it. Now sit yourself down and fill that gut so we can at least hear what everyone has do say without your stomach interrupting." Vidor's grin was teasing. Haul slid in the sit next to Caddock and filled a plate with pies and set to. He moaned in the throes of orgasmic delight, only to be startled from his meal when everyone at the table laughed long and loud. He at least had the grace to blush to the roots of his hair when he realized why, which caused another round of laughter.

Renfrew didn't speak. The abundant auburn hair dancing around his body brushed lightly over everyone at the table before he sat next to Celyn. He filled his own plate and flagon to quell his hunger. There was no time to break fast in their rush to get back to the palace from their trip to the family seat. Trahaearn was feeding in one of the many galleys placed throughout the palace. He was not required to attend such staff meetings being the younger son. Besides, all he desired was to be aimed at the enemy. He could care less about the rest.

As the edge wore off their hunger Renfrew and Haul's hair settled and braided itself in a loose rope over their shoulders. Gossip was passed along to the newcomers. Haul laughed loudly at Folant's audacity, considering Branwen outranked him and could now retaliate. He also wondered if he could convince some of the Cadre to allow him to train with them on occasion and his father stated if it ever came about he better not forget the rest of the family. They shared a momentary connection when they gazed across the table at each other, that raised the hair on everyone's neck. The tableau was broken when the next arrivals came into the room.

Baronet Macsen came in nearly buried in a synthetic fur lined, muskie coat that had a hood covering the bright ruby red hair. Mila was quick to assist, ridding him of the heavy drape and rushed away. The current Commander of Disturbance Investigations was wearing a thick woolen sweater tunic similar to Vidor's in white. His slacks were black and heavy muskie and the knee high boots he wore were faux fur lined, the shaggy tops cuffed. Macsen was very fair. His eyes were a luminous topaz with long thick eyelashes, that captivated everyone. He was well within his fifty winters with four wives at home, one only recently wed. He had four gifted children even though two of his wives were supposedly without magic and were from the merchant class instead of nobility. He always joked he would never be without clothing or food on the table since their parents were milliners and bakers. He wore a white scarf, binding his long hair at his back, and thick black dearhart gloves covered his hands beneath the sleeves of the sweater to his elbows. He smiled and greeted everyone with a handshake. Macsen was post-cognitive by touch. He needed to refrain from too much skin on skin contact with those outside of his family in order to function coherently.

As a child he spent many rotations in the University while scientists and teachers struggled to teach him to survive his acute sensibility without plunging into madness. Now he had another year and half as the director of the crime detection unit of Daear before he could return full time to his family and revel in being able to touch safe minds and motives. Macsen took his seat by Haul. The young Gifted was very soothing to be around and Macsen enjoyed his wild sense of humor. Mila came in after he was seated and tucked a thick blew around his shoulders. He gave her a beaming smile that left her blushing and sprinting from the room. There was much teasing about being the biggest flirt in the city and the atmosphere lightened even more.

Baron Colwyn strolled in next with his brother Nardo. The latter wobbled and swayed his way to the table, goblet already in hand, drunk off his head as usual. He sat next to Renfrew and ignored everyone as was typical. Colwyn offered up his own gruff hallo and sat next to Macsen.

Colwyn's younger brother Nardo had inherited his barony from his mother's cousin. It was well known gossip fodder that Nardo got it because the cousin thought he was not gifted despite the eyes. Cowyn's middle brother, Gavin, had the typical auburn hair, but all three of them had very unusual eyes, topaz with a black ring around the outside of the iris. Colwyn and Gavin had already fathered gifted children. Gavin's children driving everyone to distraction with their tendency to start fires when upset. Nardo was never sober enough to notice anyone unless it was to demand more drink. No one could even remember it being said he was other than celibate. The two black haired brothers could have passed for twins if Colwyn did not have a full beard streaked with grey. Nardo wore a goatee and mustache. They were both dressed in golden brown tunic, slacks and brown boots.

Baron Meinrad came in, perpetual sneer more intense as he attempted to get away from gesticulating Baronet Folant. The ill-tempered noble finally turned and snapped at the man, causing him to gulp in astonishment and look like a gaping fish. Mila appeared to take Meinrads' cloak and the embarrassed Folant cast his ire upon the young lady. Which refocused the attention of Meinrad onto him again. The personages at the table viewed the entire incident in silence because it was well known Meinrads' tongue was a razor sharp blade which he used with no regard to station, sex or intention. What surprised the table was the Baron then turning to the young lady and bowing over her hand leaving a small kiss on her knuckles. For the third or maybe fourth time that day Cadet Mila's face was rosy. She nodded in grateful confusion and fled. Folant, affronted or more likely embarrassed, disappeared at the same moment into the corridor. Grins were hard to hide when Meinrads' face heated, realizing everyone was paying close attention. He scowled even worse and took his seat at the table pouring cider and frowned into the cup. His face rather matched his crimson tunic.

"I do not see why correcting that ill-mannered lout's behavior is the subject of such attention.", he growled. His pale yellow eyes stood out like lamps against the tanned skin and sun bleached light brown hair.

"Perhaps you are already casting about for your next wife

Meinsy." Tensi could not help but tease. It was like breathing for her.

"Well if I am, rest assured it will never be you."

Tensi, Macsen and Haul lit the room with laughter once more.

"Rest assured. I will jump off the Queen's highest tower if that dawn ever arrives."

"Never fear, I will be happy to push you."

Even Celyn snorted at that snide remark. Before things could escalate to more amusement, Folant returned with the last member of the contingent, Baroness Pandrau, Chief of Security for the palace and all who occupy it with the exception of the sovereign.

She had the dark patina common within the FreeSouls, however her curly dark hair was worn mid back and she was able to communicate fully with all gifted. She was tall, with wide shoulders but slim torso and hips. She wore slacks at all times. For the meeting she wore the palace guard's standard uniform, a light blue tunic with the Milky Way galaxy logo. The slacks and flat heeled calf boots matched.

As was typical of the nobility there was no obvious sign of her rank in the guards. She held the authority, but outside of Daear, no one would be able to tell that at a glance. It was enough that the gifted could not be hidden without singling out the leaders with badges of office. She gave a nod to the table as a whole, only pausing at Celyn who was back to recording whatever information had him so engrossed. She glanced at Branwen, who gave her a nod. Her coils was still threaded into the young man's hair, so Pandrau knew he was being watched over. There was many grieving in the palace and the city since the last battle and her people were keeping an eye out for despairing survivors seeking more severe releases from their pain. The city's healers remained on high alert.

With one last glance over the room, she walked around the table and sat next to Meinrad. It was the least she could do to keep the peace during this meeting. Mila returned topping off the pitchers, replacing the emptied platters of pies and checking to make sure the damp towels were remaining warm and moist.

"The Queen is on her way down. Is there anything else you require Captains?"

Vidor took a survey of the room and responded.

"You have been exceptionally attentive to us today Cadet Mila. We thank you for your courtesy and patience."

"It is my pleasure to serve Captain. If you have further need of me, only advise the Queen I will be allowed to return. May your efforts insure peace for our people." She bowed to everyone and departed.

Everyone stood and stretched, walked back and forth to get their circulation going again. Meetings didn't last very long. BrightLance surprised everyone, once again, by continuing to be blunt and plain speaking. They would handle business and be gone. It was the gathering that took time. With so many wounded and others doing double duty it was a miracle everyone did show up today.

Folant walked in and went directly to a seat one over from Colwyn, after tugging his lightweight tan brocade coat tighter around him. The glitter of the metallic thread woven though out the garment pleased him greatly. It was full length and Folant believed it flattered his looks and lent an air of importance at meetings like this. He would not sit across from Meinrad, who turned his nose up like something smelled disgusting. Folant was sure Tesni had told everyone in the room of his approach to Branwen so he was hard put to keep from cringing in mortification.

Since she was the leader of her family he didn't see any reason why she should take offense about his contractual request. The Baron was wandering the wastelands instead of minding his estate and left her in charge. Who else should he speak to? Certainly not that nondescript husband number three, who spent all day questioning how much money the Quartermaster unit was spending. As if he would embezzle money from the Crown or allow his workers to get away with such a thing.

You would think he was the gifted one the way he strolled around poking into everyone's affairs. It was really unforgivable that he had to put up with such nonsense.

Folant sniffed, his hands fluttered for a moment torn between stroking his goatee or making sure his swept back, brown greying hair was still in place.

Celyn peeked at him and hid his grimace behind his hand. Honestly the man was so stuck up. He was a quartermaster, which was an important job, but it was not the same as risking his life in battle as all these men had done at one time or another. He felt choked up again and wanted only for this to be over so he could return to his quarters and the privacy he desperately needed. Branwen increased her caresses, and comforting suggestions slipped into the young man's thoughts and he once again relaxed.

A chime rang softly indicating the Queen was actually

coming in. Everyone came to attention and turned to face the metallic hatch in the back of the room. With a hiss the door slide to one side and BareBlade in all his menacing glory walked into the room and swept the interior with his piercing gaze. Behind him the five armored Cadre on guard duty entered the room and immediately shifted into position around the area as the lighting dimmed and shadows filled the perimeter of the room.

Talon entered next his tall broad body in sharp contrast to BareBlade and the guards. Today his 'blind' eyes swept the room for his own satisfaction. It was only a moment and the Queen stepped from behind him. With a smile that dazzled the unwary, she nodded to everyone and took the seat at the head of the table. She sat within Talon's shadow as he stood behind her chair, those baleful eyes once again hidden. Everyone settled themselves giving the young monarch their full attention.

The nobility could not help but look upon her with some bewilderment, even now. BrightLance was willowy, beautiful and every measure of refinement. Although the long sleeved gown was wool, it had been dyed a spruce shade of green, trimmed at the hem with embroidered prancing Pegasors. The heavy braid displayed over her shoulder showcased three black ribbons, one silver edged. A single golden one, representing her Chosen was entwined with them. The memory of her on the battlefield still disconcerted some of them. BareBlade was very sorry he missed her first foray into combat. After all MeekBlade had given him the personal assignment to train her in all things Cadre and as many of his own personal skills of stealth that she could master.

MeekBlade himself, never knew the extent of her capabilities. The King had not wanted to know. He only witnessed her sword practice and the taming of her Pegasor. BareBlade knew from reports that she did them all proud and because of her family's devotion to the Cadre, his people would be devoted to her. The squires were already enamored and that set well with him.

Folant fidgeted even more since the General of the Cadre sat next to him.

BareBlade inspired weak knees and racing heart. Macsen's people used his name during interrogations for the really hard heads that needed to be cracked. He was a stocky individual, shorter than even the average pure and the bright red hair of his youth did not contain one coil. The long Cadre braid was thick with ribbons and the colors stood out against the snow white hair he sported now. That and the abundance of scar tissue across chest and left shoulder, were the only indication of him not being a young man.

He went without shirt or armor the majority of days and his preferred short sword was openly displayed in a scabbard belted at the waist of his black dearhart hide pants. Knives were strapped to each thigh and carried in his boots. His eyes were an ordinary brown, but he also had a topaz ring around one pupil fueling speculation that his lack of magic was a lie. He had petitioned for admittance to the Cadre at twelve summers, rose through the ranks and been General for nearly thirty winters.

The 'Captains' suspected him of many things outside of Cadre business. But the unsubstantiated speculation that BareBlade may be able to teleport anywhere he wanted kept accusations quiet.

"Good Morn Captains. I will not hold you very long. My information regards Prince Farrell's prognosis and BareBlade has a report we all need to consider what our response should be. As you know the prince has suffered long term abuse and our Healers were shocked he was even alive. They are still supplying his body with required nutrients intravenously, although he is now eating broth and soft breads in very small portions multiple times a day. His mental condition is precarious. Dr. Payton states he is extremely empathic and feelings of pity or revulsion make him even more withdrawn.     Ferrell has come to grips with the fact that being in the hands of monsters, is not the death sentence he has been conditioned to think it would be. The best of the 'Infirmary' psychologist staff have been getting him to express artistically his experiences at the hands of his odious family. Farrell is shocking them with his candid depictions. You may be surprised to learn that although his hair has been shorn to his scalp since early childhood, it is very heavily coiled and they are completely receptive.     Strike and Shadow continue to visit and the prince is slowly adjusting to communication and sensations of comfort he has never experienced before. We have shown him pictographs that he can use to communicate since he is still not comfortable with vocalizing his needs. I must say the twins have exhibited endless patience with the young man.

Farrell has not been educated in any real sense. He is essentially illiterate, so we must fore go any formal training until his physical and mental health are proved stable. I realize we cannot put off a public appearance forever, but the longer we wait the closer we will be to having someone reasonably cognizant. I was thinking of exhibiting, with Farrell's permission of course, some of his more forthcoming paintings to let the people of Daear understand his plight as well as what they would have to endure at the hands of Fredric's pseudo government. I am very aware of the poison that maniac spews infecting segments of our own society. I will not allow it to push us into civil war. We stand as one people, we will fall as one people."

Vidor listened closely to the report and knew he could not avoid expressing his thought. The young man's presence could be used to ferment trouble in their own lands if not handled properly.

"When do the Healers believe the young man may have other visitors beyond the medical staff and Strike and Shadow? No offense my Queen, but those two are not the most compassionate duo to be around. Surely the young man must see that all of us live in comradery less he think his confinement is less than truthful."

"A very important point Captain. The hope is once his overall condition have improved he will be more receptive to investigating the world around him. He needs to have some control over his own body. Now he is still helpless as a babe. They are hopeful before the next clear sighting of Cat's Eye this will be possible. They cannot place him in a stabilizer. As you know that technology works best on open wounds. Using the device would probably be too much of a shock for his weak system and kill him. Even if we could use it for such long term damage, it would delay his mental recovery. The consensus is his mind and body must keep a pace with each other to insure we prevent despair and physical setbacks. Prince Farrell must realize that he has found security, a home where he will not be shunned but embraced by all our people."

"Will it be possible for any of us to visit with him? I think a few well timed comments when certain ears are paying attention could start the process. At this moment the Court knows nothing and speculation could do more damage than not."

"I see no reason not to see that done. I have visited, of course, speaking to him when he is aware, but oft times I just talk to his slumbering form. Dr. Payton believes he can hear during those times he is asleep at least subconsciously. Do any of you have a spare moment to be added to rotation?"

Haul snorted as he looked around the table.

"Sire and I can not. The boy would have a heart attack. I think Strike and Shadow already gave him the fright of his life. He must find out we are more than warriors. Tensi should go and Celyn. Not to add to your time here lad, but a visit or two before you began your journey would give you information to pass on to the other Baronets. It would be best if honest truth was passed on. The people are expecting a wedding and an end of strife. We hope to give them that. But we must not present a falsehood only for them to discover the Queen's consort may be rotations away or never, able to assist her rule. We were expecting one 'pure' consort blind to all magic, not a Gifted broken by torture. Our people need to know that the Gifted are being born in Haven and possibly being hidden because of the fate of the Prince. Fredric's people may fear us, but if they were free from his tyranny, the Gifted would have an alternative to living with hate."

Haul's anger stirred the hair on everyone's neck and most of them shifted in their seats wanting their weapons to hand. In moments they felt the Queen's power stir around them and a calm settled in, easing the tension. Renfrew gave his Queen a long look beneath his lashes. So the enigma had more abilities to be revealed. Perhaps everyday would bring new insight into her skills and power.

"I concur. I will be looking into his genetic makeup anyway, once the report has been received from the Infirmary. A visit would add to the overall picture." Tensi concluded.

"Ah, Tensi so cold hearted. The poor lad is more than a scientific curiosity. For shame!"

Baroness Branwen looked incensed as she admonished her friend.

Tensi did have the grace to blush.

"My apologies your Grace and everyone. I did not mean to sound like Prince Farrell's welfare was of little concern. He may technically have family among us and I could find out if they would be receptive in getting to know him no matter the connection may be distant. His young Protector Lucan did report that the entire family of his mother was executed by Fredric. I hope to discover some remnants of them here."

"I understand Baroness Tensi. I had not contemplated the prince having family here in Daear. Even the smallest possibility may assist his recovery. Baronet Celyn are you willing to delay your journey long enough to visit Prince Farrell? I know your duties are extensive now and would not delay if it stresses your family."

"Thank you my Queen. If at all possible I would like to

lcave at the fifth dawning."

Celyn had already planned to depart on that dawn. He was very nervous advising the Queen of that fact considering she was asking him personally to see her future husband. It would behoove him to remain as long as she required, but his concern for his mother and sister in law could not be ignored either.

"Never fear I will see you well on your way by the fifth dawning. I am sure the Healers can arrange a visit before that dawn."

Celyn nodded. He was relieved. He did not know his Queen well enough to be aware of what could offend her or not. He wished heatedly for this meeting to end so he could retire to his quarters. He had spent too much time close to tears and hearing the horror this man, no older than himself had gone through was not assisting his composure.

"I am not doing anything more than showing my face so the Court does not think me dead, again. I can spend time with the lad if you will it." Vidor thought it would be a good respite from his personal boredom. Even if it was just to sit by the sleeping boy and read to him. Of course, Vidor could reminisce about his own past adventures.

"I also will attend if it is your desire my Queen. Let me know when it most efficacious for my attendance and I will work it into my schedule. I have enough subordinates to cover for me for this short amount of time away." Baroness Pandrau volunteered.

"Thank you Baroness. I appreciate your assistance with Prince Farrell's recovery." BrightLance bestowed one of her dazzling smiles in the direction of the palace Chief of Security.

Pandrau was thankful for her complexion as her face heated under that smile.

"I think we should all eventually rotate in the schedule to visit. Not only will Farrell see that more females than the Queen holds authority here, but realize that our people are not segregated by our genetic makeup. I am sure the lies he has heard over his lifetime made us monsters. The more differences he sees in the beginning, the sooner he can accept the wider scope of the world. Fredric loves his people ignorant and superstitious. We will need much patience to deal with both these orphans."

Caddock's heart truly ached for the poor boy. The baron was considered a soft hearted man by most who knew him. He had wept openly at the deceased King's bedside. Everyone knew his children and wives were cosseted and fiercely protected. He was the Chosen of one of his Gifted wives which increased his desire to protect them. It was a source of amazement that Caddock could leave her side to ride into battle. His rationale was preventing the enemy from ever breaching the gates of his estate by killing them beyond the Gates of Daear.

"The Chosen Lucan has been released from medical and is resting in the Cadre's barracks. Sticker has been his constant companion, as is her way, until he is feeling more secure about his safety. She has taken him on short forays into the terraced gardens. He refuses to touch his weapons and keeps within her sight at all times when not sleeping. I fully intend to turn him over to the palace gardeners when he is no longer afraid to walk among us. Perhaps his spirit will eventually be healed. But I have no intention of having him pressed into any kind of service, not even as Chosen of Prince Farrell. For both of them, the very thought of being in the same room brings on anxiety attacks and nausea. The mere thought of Shadow and Strike leave Lucan almost catatonic in terror. We may never be able to resolve this injustice. But we will give them as much peace and isolation as we can, so they will not feel threatened."

There were sighs and nods in agreement on this decision. Both men were too fragile and would be for many rotations. They were beyond the current equations in the ongoing efforts to avert further warfare.

"General please present your report."

"Your Grace," BareBlade acknowledged the Queen, then turned his attention to the reason he accompanied her.

"We have received reports which confirm the situation in Fredric's domain is close to dissolving his so called kingdom. I think starvation will be the normal circumstances for those outside of his personal estate. He has indeed stripped the land of everything to support his troops. Even the FreeSouls are reporting incursions and they are far from Fredric's borders through one of the longest mountain passes. The Senate has sent emissaries with emergency relief. Some of them have been attacked by brigands and even the people receiving the supplies are hard put to keep them from brigands and Fredric's men. So far he has not had any of his obvious troops raid into the mountains, but the FreeSouls have increased border guards armed with the old ship blasters."

At this statement the Captain's expressions were grim and Renfrew and Haul were hard pressed to keep the anticipatory grins from their faces.

"It must be very serious if the FreeSouls are arming their

guards beyond swords and bow. It is not the usual procedure for them. We cannot afford to have the FreeSouls invaded. They will resist but their main focus has always been academic and social welfare. They do not have strategists to helm an attack force." Renfrew's surprising baritone rumbled into the room. "We are aware they are resistant to us involving ourselves in their affairs, however aid in this matter should at least be offered. If the pass is mined that would prevent incursions and loss of life for the FreeSouls. They cannot afford to lose their people to save those who have allowed Fredric to drive them into ruin."

"With the Queens's endorsement we have advised the Senate that military aid is available, however the FreeSouls must live with the decision they make in that regard. I am loath to recall our troops who have had no time to warm their own beds after this latest battle. However our own border guards along the demarcation line with the FreeSouls should have their weapon caches increased as a precaution. It may look badly of us from the FreeSoul's point of view."

BareBlades' actual thoughts were, 'to the Coils with what the FreeSoul's thought about a buildup on their borders'. For two centuries the relationship between the two settlements had been nothing less than amiable. The only bone of contention had always been the open house policy of the FreeSoul's. It was only during this latest summer of hostilities that they limited who could travel through the pass into their lands from Haven. The ongoing hostilities had become serious war instead of skirmishes, and the FreeSoul's wished to prevent being caught between the two forces. Peace was the preference.

The FreeSoul's had no wish to return to the days when 'the ships' and the colonists fought against each other. They made peace with the human hybrids in Daear and knew that the occasional influx of 'new' blood from all their other neighbors kept their own people healthy. FreeSoul's lived long and thrived. The only manifestation of 'gifts' were the rare Chosen. And the even more rare, Seers that appeared once or twice a century.

Vidor rolled his eyes at BareBlade's not quite subtle sarcasm.

"Just as we cannot force them to accept our assistance, they cannot protest us solidifying our own borders. If they protest we have amble proof of the damage subversive elements have done our people. We have foiled two assassination plots that had Captains from our own council working with Fredric's hatemongers. It is no stretch to know they would have reported on the FreeSouls as well. I know many of their people hold the same views toward us, but they prefer their isolation to bloodshed. I would not have them doing more than attempting to stop the starvation of the citizens. Their active support, lending weapons and scientific knowledge would be ill for us."

"We cannot afford to lose the FreeSouls as a passive ally. The gene pool would not be diversified enough with them eliminated through war." As always Tensi's thoughts were on the larger picture of a healthy fertile population.

"Let us not forget that although considered few in number, the Gifted of Daear level out the other's ability to cause too much attrition. To put it bluntly, if threatened we know the predator in all of us will awaken. I personally do not want to know what I would become if I had to fight at the gates of my estate to protect my family." The Baron Caddock scowled as he spoke and his ire stirred the more sensitive of the Gifted in the room.

Everyone shifted uneasily at Caddock's pronouncement. Colwyn was nodding in agreement for although he and his brothers were considered weakly gifted with little overt abilities, the Baron was not unaware of the lust for carnage that rode his spirit when he fought. There had been occasions where those thought without talents would express such powers when under duress. It was enough that he was wary of Nardo's possible talents erupting during battle, though no evidence existed of there being any.

Baron Vidor poured himself another cider and drank deeply. He really did not need the news of possible trouble with the FreeSouls.

"Put fear into the spies by having a troop of Cadre show up along the borders. The FreeSouls will not be happy once it is reported, but the troop will catch us a few infiltrators. The others will retreat. Fredric cannot support any serious forays into our territory with his own people desperate and weak. In the mean time we reinforce our garrisons with blasters and use some of the infrared detectors in the less traveled passes. We only need to put eight additional men per garrison to constantly monitor those detectors once installed. They would have been rotated in as regular replacements at the beginning of summer anyway. A few months early will not be a problem and the extra numbers will not be noted if the Cadre makes enough noise."

"Noise," BareBlades laughed. "You want the Cadre to

make noise. I will have to retrain my people after rotations of bashing them in the head to be quiet. But I do not have a problem with that idea. It will be good stealth practice to have them install the detectors under cover of night and ride roaring Pegasors up and down the passes during the day scaring away Fredric's rabble."

"It is not a bad idea at all. I consider it a very low key response to the situation. My first inclination was to volunteer my sons and I to check some of the not often used trails over the mountains. I do realize that too many Gifted appearing on the borders would panic the FreeSouls. Sadly I must restrain myself and attend to the dull business of estate management," Renfrew's maniacal grin widened. "Unless something unexpected occurs and the Cadre could use our assistance?"

BareBlade scowled, but he could not hold it long and finally matched Renfrew's grin.

"Have no doubt, if 'something' unusual happens I will not hesitate to press you into service sir."

"Good, good. I would not desire to be remiss in the duties to Queen and country."

It was BrightLance that snorted at Renfrew's comment. Before anyone else would think it was ill mannered for him to speak in such sarcastic tone.

"I am very aware sir that what most consider odious and dangerous business, skulking around in ill-reputed locals is your great joy. Especially if there is someone for you to fight. I promise if I discover any reason for you to flit about the land uncovering illicit activities, I will rush a message to you immediately.

All this was said with the Queen's winning smile,

however Renfrew received the serious promise behind it leaving him to expect just such a missive to keep him busy.

"My Queen. I am your servant in all things and I thank you from the bottom of my hearts."

BrightLance blushed and laughed.

"Renfrew you and your sons must be the only people in Daear that cheer when I say go risk you necks."

"Here, here my Queen. Just point me," Haul saluted with a laugh and toasted BrightLance before upending his flagon in a long series of swallows.

"This is all the information we have for now. I am pleased we have a consensus on how to address the situation. I look forward to seeing you during your visits to Farrell. Thank you Captains."

The Captains rose as one and bowed to the Queen. The meeting had come to a prosperous conclusion. It was rare that there was not some bone of contention over tactics. The common thought was the betrayal at their own table and the subsequent battles had momentarily quelled the contentiousness with which the monarchs often had to contend with.

BareBlade was the first to depart, followed by two of the shadowed guards. The Queen followed with Talon covering her back. The remaining guards stood watch until the Captains were assisted into their cloaks by the returned Mila and ushered from the room. Mila sealed the hatch and the guards followed her out into the Queens domain. The trio took up their places in the dark halls below her quarters.

# Beneath CatsEye

Farrell crept across the stones to the floor to ceiling window that was a wall of his room. The vista spread out before him always drew him back whenever the care givers departed. His shaky legs and tender feet scarcely supported his body as he fell against the padded lounge and crawled upon it. After a breathless scrambling and shoving aside his very own art books, Farrell managed to prop himself against the scattered fat green pillows that supported his back and head. He was exhausted, but he did not remember a time when he was not. The care giver had returned him to bed for sleep, but the expanse beyond the window was a lure he could not suppress. The young prince scrubbed his face against the soft brushed fabric that covered his pillows. 'Pillows' were made from an odd springy substance the care givers called 'foam'. He thought clouds must feel like this floating across the sky dawn and dark, so comfortable to lie upon.

He gradually situated himself beneath the pale green blew that warmed him and turned his eyes to the mountain crags. Frost covered the outside edges of the window and he could see the deep grey surface give way to a wide terrace beneath it. There were big 'telescopes' there, which the demons said circled the mountain and allowed one to see beyond the clouds to look at the 'stars'. The demons had promised to take him one dark to see those 'stars'. The idea continued to fill him with awe. He was told they looked close enough to touch, especially CatsEye which shown light into this window at night and was not a 'moon' but a 'planet' like Nadredd. Since he lived on Nadredd, Nadredd was a planet. Farrell was very confused about that explanation. What was a moon?

Below that ledge another terrace extended. There were small buildings there but he had no idea what they were for. There were multiple ledges some wide and others narrow further down the mountainside. It was fascinating to discover plants of some type growing on a few of them. Others supported long tables and chairs and sometime lounges. He could even see, far off below and to the right, those fierce Pegasor creatures running across a wide paddock sometimes wrestling each other to the ground. They were beautiful. Farrell fully intended to paint them running around so free. He shivered a little at that thought. The Pegasors chased dearhart across the same area and fought over the kills. What fierce creatures they were. He would not watch them eat dearhart. It made him cry.

Farrell had been aware for almost sixty dawns. He continued to spend many hours sleeping. Occasionally he painted watery pictures of the images in his head because the Healers stated doing so would assist his recovery by 'expressing' his experience. He was not sure why he should 'recover' or 'express', but he had performed as ordered all his life, so now would not dare disobey the demons. Sometimes he mused on 'concern', another new sensation and word, they lavished on him. These demons were really strange. They had not killed him. They gave him 'medicine', which did not let him vomit or scream when he was frightened. Farrell was frightened all the time.

The Healers praised him for eating the little bowls of food and drinking water. Everyone wanted to touch his head with their own hair, if they had the long kind that moved! Everyone had hair, short or long and a few had red or 'auburn' colors. That new color word was confusing because 'auburn' seemed to have many variations of red or brown. He had not been able to accurately duplicate the color on the pictures he painted. It was bad enough daring to sneak peeks at the demons. Painting with shaky hands earned him praise from them, even though his pictures were mostly swirls of colors mashed together. Now he could not make 'auburn' no matter how much he mixed red and brown. Some of his old servants had no hair on their heads. They were normal people. Farrell had never seen a bald demon. Demons were abominations.

It was really scary when the demon 'twins' or the demon Queen arrived in the outer rooms. The bristles on his own head stood on end and waved around. The sensation made him sick. He wanted to scream and beg for the clippers. When he cried he was told he would get used to the strange feeling of his hair wiggling! That was supposed to be normal! When the twin's hair caressed his head Farrell felt such odd sensations. It was explained that he was given 'sanctuary' and that meant 'safety'. He was unsure what that could mean for his 'future', which was also a strange concept. The twins introduced him to 'comfort' also. He was just managing to understand the tenuous connection between the new words and 'feelings'. Farrell looked at the scattered clouds drifting by as the sky dawn colors of azure and cream darkened to emerald and a scary grey. He went to sleep on the lounge reciting the names of sky colors he remembered from his color charts.

Caregiver Keyla returned to the room to light the globes and discovered Farrell asleep on the lounge for the second time. He was displaying disobedience. It would please everyone on staff after the first forty dawnings cowering in his bed when awake. Keyla ignited only a few globes around the medical bunk, straightened the covers, then added an extra blew to his slumbering body. His books were re-stacked neatly beside his temporary bed and the lap easel was filled with new paper. The completed paintings were collected from the side table and floor to give to the Healers.

She cleaned his brushes and replaced the dirty water with clean for his paint box. Keyla checked his wrist monitor to confirm the standard readings and left the room as stealthily as she entered. The little prince was easily startled. Everyone was extra careful to avoid the flashbacks to beatings and verbal tirades he had endured when his very existence was otherwise being ignored. She gave one last glance at Farrell hoping his deep sleep would last through the night. It would be the first time and another level in his healing.

\*\*\*

While Farrell dreamed of water colors and demon's writhing hair, Lucan sat on the terrace of the Cadre Infirmary watching CatsEye lift into the night sky. It glowed orange like aged cheese with a dark striation cutting it nearly in half. Sometimes the lower portion of the planet's surface could not be seen at all, but the impression of its perimeter remained visible. For now Lucan was as relaxed as possible on thick cushions and wearing one of his mentor's big woolen shirts. Sticker was in a meeting with her company and the Healers of the Cadre were on duty. No one could approach him without going through the formidable males that made up the medical unit. Lucan had learned not to fear the Healers.

Most of the Cadre seemed not to be much different from himself. He still could not bear the sight of Strike and Shadow, however. Their strange gold eyes stripped him naked and the writhing hair evoked horrible images of how those soldiers might have died in their attempt to kill the young prince. Terror was an understatement when one day he discovered Brace and Fewfingers sitting on a bench talking after a weapons practice. Strands of their hair lifted from the tight Cadre braid and twisted together in the space between them. They wiped the sweat from their face and shoulders while laughing and maligning each other's prowess.

Sticker explained that even if some could not perform magic, they could communicate in that manner. She assured him that she and quite a few others did not have that capability. It disturbed him that the formidable warrior expressed some envy of those able to speak to the Gifted.

Most days he was Sticker's shadow. He slept in her arms still, to his embarrassment, and sometimes had panic attacks if she remained at a distance for too long. He was taking short excursions on his own to the terraced flower and vegetable gardens. It made his heart ache to see such beauty and abundance when his lands were filled with the dead and starving. The Queen had met with him on two occasions, advising him of the FreeSoul's efforts to aid his people. He wept before her, ashamed at his weakness and the cruelty of Fredric to his own people.

He ruminated over the past as he knew it, attempting to reconcile the history as recorded by the demons. Lucan had been given free access to the small Cadre depository, marveling at the 'computers' and discs that contained information. Sticker sat with him as he read through the pages on the screen, until she forced him away to rest.

Before Fredric's grandfather, Haven had been a loose association of people that kept to themselves and traded with the Rovers on the rare times the wanderers entered their domain. Haven by tradition did not have diplomatic relations with the FreeSouls and certainly not with the demons. Rovers were considered of 'pure' stock. When they fled the military rule the wanderers vowed to never settle for any form of government having dominion over themselves. Nadredd's environment was the only master they acknowledged and they survived within it's confines. Rover trade flourished with Haven until Cort Brooks, raised the question of Rovers being spies for the demons. This was spurred by the rumors of abundance in Daear and a flourishing city called Stara, which was within the mountain stronghold of FreeSouls. Compared with endless labor and rationing that was often a fact in Haven, envy soon took poisonous root. Eventually Rovers found less welcome and sometimes open hostility. Trade became confined to the borderlands where the people were more isolated and independent of Cort's efforts to unite the settlers.

Cort eventually raised the ire of the people reminding them of the unauthorized experiments on their ancestors and contorted monsters found in the labs before they fled. Not only were the Rovers spies, but Daear intended to attack and gain more people for their evil subjugation. His campaign took many rotations but by the time Fredric was born, his father Lorne was gathering soldiers and demanding an end to the demons beyond the mountains. For the first time 'taxes' were levied and people accepted the burden of supporting an army to take back what was rightfully theirs.

The first forays by Lorne's troops through FreeSoul's territory was met with surprising resistance. If Haven's men had approached without visible weapons, they would have passed unopposed considering the FreeSoul's acknowledged pacifism. But armed men, resembling a mob more than a disciplined group, sent up every alarm. The mountain crags protected the border guards from retaliation by his foot soldiers as they held the high ground. The retreat of the 'army' was an embarrassment for the self-styled king.

Lorne turned his attention directly to Daear after an unexpected encounter with a group of exploring Searchers traveling through unclaimed land. A lone messenger hawk carried the news of the assault back to Daear. Not one member of the Searcher group survived. That was the first time Cadre went beyond the mountains searching for survivors and then evidence of their fate, which they discovered.

Daear sent dispatches demanding justice, Haven did not respond and the messenger hawks eventually ceased to be sent. Instead, a show of arms evolved at the bottom of the mountainside. The llygredd gave a swift agonizing response to the Haven scouts hoping to sneak near enough to the first great gate and plant explosives. One guard of Daear was killed when they went out the next morning to recover the bodies being unaware of the devices the scouts had carried. The people demanded action and Cadre went into the field as a show of force. Skirmishes occurred through the rotations, circumvented often my Nadredd's capricious weather patterns. The task of defeating the demons fell to the subjects of Fredric reinforced by the mix of historical fact and the current fiction the creatures wanted the people of Haven to occupy their demon labs.

Lucan had been promised by the Queen that he would not be conscripted into their military units or forced to see young Farrell again, if he did not wish it. Even now Lucan emotions overflowed in shame and that strange ache at the thought of the poor child. He had the concept of Chosen explained to him. It still left him dismayed and sickened to be considered a companion of a demon. What could he possibly do for a broken starved boy, who could still possibly die from the rotations of abuse? Lucan could not wrap his mind around it. All that was left was a hallow sense of pain that assaulted him severely at random moments.

Lucan was very surprised to be offered an assignment in the Agricultural Guild, which included care of the terraced gardens along the cliffs. Lucan admitted he remembered little of the teachings of his father after so many rotations among the rough men that patrolled Haven's borders and slipped into the forest below Daear to scout. The Queen told him the supervisor of the gardens was a Gifted. If he was too uncomfortable working with the woman, they would make the effort to find him something else to do. Perhaps he would like to live in the city and attend the University to discover an unrealized talent? Lucan found the generosity overwhelming, even suspicious. But for now he only had to rest, and rest some more then wait for Sticker to come and take him to her bed.

\*\*\*

Raze watched the man climb around the boulders and rock in the dark. CatsEye was bright tonight and aided her already excellent vision. He thought to be quiet, to slip pass the patrols of Cadre that suddenly appeared on the cliffs.

Pegasors roared and snarled throughout the day giving fair warning to trespassers of their intent to maim anything considered prey. The Cadre had mined some of the least known trails into Daear's lands and made a show of force at the outposts on the FreeSoul's border. Their presence covered the arrival of reinforcements and weapons to each one. Strike and Shadow made a point to be seen by FreeSoul's counterparts. Inspiring hysteria when they would appear, Pegasors prancing and coils floating in the air about them. Raze snickered imagining the reports back to FreeSoul headquarters.

This man was dressed like a simple farmer but he moved

too stealthily. She would win a bet that he was wearing some form of protection under those filthy rags. He certainly did not move like a starving man. Most of the people in Haven were malnourished now, unless they were the elite basking in Fredric's approval. The self-styled King of Haven expanded his lands to accommodate his army of murderers and thieves. They preyed on their own people more often than they ever did on anyone else.

Raze was not political. Diplomacy was wasted time when your enemy could be dying. She was moved by one fierce devotion, the kill, and praise for her skills in the accomplishment. Raze knew from childhood that she was different, detached from affection and devotion that her family prized so much. She just did not feel those things for anyone. The Cadre gave her focus, to train hard, for the few ecstatic days she would be set free to end a life. She preened when her commanders praised her abilities and worked diligently to control herself when orders required she not kill. That was her hardest test, to not fail an order so the Cadre would keep her. She was intelligent enough to know that outside of their environs, the Cadre would have been assisting Disturbance Investigations to end her life. As long has the Cadre embraced her the civilians of Daear were safe.

Oh, the man fell down. Raze shook with silent amusement as he rolled back the way he had climbed, landing with a thump. He would be disoriented now, perfect. The shock of the fall had him cursing under his breath, a clarification of his true status and intentions. A person on innocent business would be cursing quite loudly or yelling in pain, if they had breath after a fall like that. Everyone knew the forest creatures rarely trespassed into the mountain passes. At least the FreeSouls did not hesitate to kill snakes.

Raze moved away from her perch, her blew wrapped feet settling lightly on the rubble strewn stone. The idiot had rolled to his back and lay attempting to catalog his injuries. CatsEye's brilliant light did not illuminate all areas of the narrow pass, but it was a captivating sight in the space above the man's head.

The Cadre warrior checked him over to be sure he was still alive and stripped him of blades and a packet that may contain important correspondence, or his lunch for all she cared. Only the Commanders would be interested in what it contained. It had been so easy, just pick up a rock and smack him in the head. She opened his coat and did find an ancient Kevlar vest that would have stopped a blaster on a low setting. Too bad for him rocks worked better than blasters in some situations. She supposed she would have to take him back to the outpost for questioning. How many vests did these thieves have?

As she surmised, he was too well fed too be a common man. It only took a few minutes to strip him and contain his movements in magnetic bands on wrist and ankles. Raze sealed his eyes and mouth shut with the liquid bandage. The stuff worked so well for things like this. She always filched some from the medical stores when it was time to hunt. She whistled softly and her Pegasor rose up from behind a large wall of rock and padded to her side. The mare stood patiently, as Raze dragged the man across the ground and heaved him onto her back. It took a moment longer to clip the saddle rings to the magnetic bands so he could not slide off. The

Pegasor padded after her like an obedient pet when Raze headed up the pass. The mare had a full belly for once and would remain docile until her hunger rose again. Raze considered the possibilities of being allowed attendance during the questioning, but it was more likely the twins would be there to make quick work of the process. Ah well, maybe next time.

*** 

Alanah gathered up her grey skirt in one hand and climbed the stairs to Verna's bedroom. Her ankle boots felt like lead weights hanging off the ends of her legs. Faylynn and Garnet were finally asleep, wrapped tightly around each other in a quest for mutual comfort and security. It had taken two stories to settle the excitable little girls down after their day of rambunctious antics. Alanah was very tired. She still had three months of pregnancy ahead of her and the task of supervising day to day operations around the estate. The Queen promised to send a court accountant to assist her and the family after their husband's shocking betrayal. Verna had been confined to bed by the Cadre Healer. She was cowed by the stern armored man who tethered her to intravenous bags for the duration of his stay at their estate.

The thought of the marriage that brought her parents so much pride now filled Alanah with shame. Traitors, the family of two and the last of their line, traitors to Daear and the Captain's Council. Their children's honored ancestry would be forever tainted by the despicable actions of their father. It was impossible to know if the oldest daughter or the son she carried would ever be allowed to sit at the Captain's table after this horrible season passed.

First there was Verna's failing health when she had always been exceptionally robust. Then the University being attacked and Cadre arriving in force to drag her husband, Kane, away for interrogation and eventual execution. A Healer in the unit had taken one look at Verna's weakened state and examined her on the spot. He found poison. It was just enough to slow her down and impact her immune system. Eventually Verna would have taken to her bed and died, perhaps a year from now. Alanah almost went into labor caused by so many shocks and disappointments.

The Cadre had remained, searching the estate and questioning all the retainers. Macsen had been requested and the Gifted had come with lawyers from Disturbance Investigation. Several of their guard were taken away to the Palace and not returned. After many hours of questioning she and Verna had been cleared of wrong doing. The little girls had seen the Healer and been declared free of dangerous substances. Alanah was quick to get an examination and prayed for her child to be healthy. It was a relief to know they were all safe, but Alanah requested sanctuary for the remaining family, as they would be defenseless without anyone to trust. Surely the relatives of the dead from the University assault would be seeking revenge?

The blessing in the midst of this horror was the news of Kane's possible attempts to kill his wives and his Gifted babies spread, and was being met with public outrage. Vernas's two little girls, age five and two were telekinetic, a not uncommon magic. The youngest was rather delicate, but it was possible that would change as she aged. Alanah suspected Newlyn would be a strong telepath because her unborn child was touching her thoughts after he sensed all the upset. For the most part she felt his confusion and agitation. She made every effort to sooth him, though she was did not have any magic to touch his little mind.

She took one last peek into Verna's room before arriving at her own door. Her friend slept peacefully, the coarse mass of brown hair tightly braided and pinned atop her head by the Healer. Once inside her own room Alanah removed the sweater and pulled the laces apart on her blew skirt. She refused to bother putting them away tonight. The bathing chamber was steps away but Alanah was too tired for even that.

She pushed the covers back and dived in still wearing her long johns. She almost let go the hysterical laughter that haunted her mind, but muffled a giggle into her pillow. It was so good to still be able to sleep in her own bed. She dragged a pillow down to rest between her knees and fell asleep rubbing her Newlyn bump.

Stave kept to the shadows, patrolling the first floor of former Baron Kane's hall, double checking all entry points were secure. No one knew if any co-conspirators remained in the vicinity and it was urgent that the remaining family survive this debacle. It had been lucky chance the Baroness Verna and her family had been detained during the day. Her wan complexion and shadowed eyes would have probably gone unremarked as distress by torchlight. The shock of finding poison, and such a slow acting one had literally stunned him. It would be a few months before she was back to full health. Until then, he would remain with Dump to treat her and protect the family.

No one would consider Stave a healer on first glance. He didn't fit the ideal like Talisman did. Stave was tall and big boned like many pure, with dark brown hair cut close to his scalp, except for the braid. He had a grim visage even good humor would not crack. He earned his name because of all the heads he broke with the walking stick he was never seen without. A length of oak, it was now wrapped in strips of Cadre ribbons, adhering to the stick with blood from opponents, friendly and otherwise. That 'stick' had come with his entry into the Cadre squires. It was his weapon of choice for most fights, but he was not hesitant to weld sword and short blades. All the warrior vanished, however, when a patient was in need. He was gentle, without expressing a 'bedside manner.' He always stated if patients wanted to be coddled they could have Talisman and the other healers take care of them. If they wanted to be healed and go on their way, he was the man for the job.

Stave moved silently through the large home, admiring the art on the walls, the carefully dyed drapes at the windows and the thick hand woven rugs that provided warmth on the cold stone floors. It still shocked him that a man of Kane's standing would throw away such a life of important work and fine family. Especially for reasons that were so far back in their history and could not be changed. He knew he was no more pure than any human living on Nadredd. To be truly pure was to risk death just for walking too long in the now oxygen rich air. You could never tell with Nadredd. Things mutated. No one knew why the Origin Earth type planet had that oddity.

The mad Fredric was ignoring selected bits of the first landfall histories. He ranted about experiments and disregarded the first shocking revelation the colonist faced. They had been lied to. Panicked people turned on each other. The colony ships were filled with those Origin Earth wanted rid of and their descendants. They were fated to die slowly from the air or by the sneaking predators that they did not realize were there. The Healer sent another urgent appeal into the Universe for the endless strife over the past to end.

Stave even mused over possible alternate histories for himself as he walked. If he had not dedicated his life to the Cadre, the strong willed women the traitor abandoned would have made ideal wives. The pregnant one was most compelling. She oversaw the labor of the retainers. She also kept an eye on the maids and cared for the little girls. He made sure to remind her to rest often during the day, but she was a stubborn one.

Sooner than the women may desire, loyal men would have to be found to replace the estate guards who turned out to be Fredric's people smuggled in as Searchers. Gossip was, Baron Meinrad was on the lookout for a new wife. The man had a bitter disposition if ever there was one, but he was a fierce fighter and could hold the estate until the children were old enough to decide whether to retake their father's bloodied seat. No reason to bring the subject up, Meinrad and the other barons would be lurking about soon enough. Caddock may even show up in person, considering Alanah was supposed to be a cousin. That man would insure the women remained free from pressure. Perhaps he should send a message.

Stave choked back the chuckle at the thought of old

Vidor pressing his suit. The man was a legend and probably still as fertile as coils were plentiful on the twins' heads. He thought it may be a curse, however, to love so many and have time take them from you. Then go on with no end in sight. Something happened to the Fleet Admiral and the Generals on that journey. There was nothing to be found which explained the longevity in the archives, but the sky above kept the secret.

Ah well, time to go up and poke Bump to take his place patrolling the house. He would have to be at his best, to sneak up on the skinny walking stick that was his comrade in arms. Pale complexioned and heavily freckled, Bump looked like a swift wind would blow him over. Gossip was he could hear clouds moving in the sky. Yet Bump insisted that he only paid attention. He chided all Cadre for not performing to his level, so training included stalking the boney man. The squires were not the only ones collecting bruises for sneak attacks on Bump. Hopefully Stave would not collect any waking Bump tonight. It would be embarrassing and get regaled around the barracks by the laughing old warrior.

He took a last look out into the courtyard checking the guards on the walls. They had taken the admonishment to keep to the shadows to heart. It would be difficult tonight as CatsEye was large and dark gold, reminding him of Alanah's hair.

\*\*\*

The rising sun battled CatsEye for dominance of the lightening sky. Barely visible fog seeped into the dark until the planetoid's gold was a hazy shimmer behind building dismal green clouds instead of azure sky. They would continue to build over the sea and bring icy rain. Soon the tornadoes and windstorms would be master of the planet for the winter. Daear and the surrounding estates would be sheltered by the high mountains from the worst of it.

Near the top of the Palace, BrightLance stood on her terrace breathing in the brisk clean air. The breeze lifted her unbraided hair chilling her scalp and raising chill bumps along her neck and shoulders.

The gardeners should be up today to move the windflowers indoors. Pink was definitely not her favorite shade. Tomorrow she would have the preferred winter pansies brightening the terrace.

She feared winter was arriving early once again. It pleased her to know foodstuffs had been stored from the last two season's harvest. This season fonio had dominated the greenhouses and they managed three harvests. Half of the abundance would be stockpiled. It was explained to her long ago that Nadredd eventually orbited far from its sun and darkness would dominate the land for a time. Her people would be prepared. Survival was the end and beginning of practically every action on Nadredd. The upside of this would be more metal for her people as well, for the FreeSouls would trade well for the excess grains they could not grow in their tunnels.

BrightLance had been up for four bells completing her meditations and warm-up exercises. Today she would have a light breakfast and report to BareBlade's private sanctum to be put through his idea of training. It had been seven dawnings since she had last reported. He was going to "beat her skinny ass into shape, because having administrative duties was no excuse for not honing her skills in some form every day!" At least she was passed the point where she would cry or rave about his harsh workouts. The people of Daear were depending on her to protect them. She could not do that if she allowed herself to become weak and dependent on others to protect her person.

Mila set off the motion detector as she approached the hatch to the Queen's private quarters. Another chime announced her presence when she pushed the cart, laden with a meal and reports, into the bedroom. The door onto the terrace opened and a stiff breeze lifted her already fluffy curls. BrightLance stepped in wearing her Cadre black tunic and slacks, sans boots.

"Good morning Mila. I hope I did not disturb your rest so early this dawning."

"Oh no my Queen. I was well rested from my down time, thank you. I have the latest news available for your attention and a light repast as you requested."

BrightLance sat herself down at the dainty little table near the windowed wall as Mila placed her small goblet of soup and saucer of thin crackers before her. She sipped and ate crackers with one hand while she flipped the pages of flimsies and paper notes. Mila straightened her bed and laid out the elaborate gown she would wear to court after she rested four bells. Luncheon with her ladies in waiting would be next on the agenda. During lunch she would become aware of the gossip permeating the Palace. Then her long afternoon and evening of listening to petitioners from the city, the

Ambassadors from the FreeSouls and various department head's harangue. By the time all that was done BrightLance would be happy to have remained in BareBlade's company.

The Queen observed Mila moving about the room and contemplated marriage proposals. Mila was attractive and the interaction she had with the Barons was not disregarded. Meinrad was indeed looking for a wife. For all his sour disposition in public, his wives were well educated, contributing to the community. One was a Veterinarian, the other an Instructor of Basics. Word was they grieved the loss of the third wife but appeared to be recovering well. He would be a good husband for an engineering student and Mila was attracted to him. But then she was attracted to most of the Barons. They were a well turned out group. Vidor still cut a fine figure. Oddly enough Haul paid her no mind at all. The handsome heir had quite the reputation, but kept his physical needs confined to the most exclusive brothel. His manners with the ladies of court was impeccable. She would have to consider this more. Once the Council saw she was fully capable of making difficult decisions, they would be less sure of their influence on her. They could consider marriage not be worth the bother. Perhaps a word at lunch could draw some attention to Mila.

By the time breakfast was eaten, CatsEye's gold was being obscured by bilious green grey clouds. BrightLance was sure that next dawning would bring more rain. She had hopes for a peaceful winter. Her people needed it. The treat from Haven could not be allowed to continue and some very hard choices would have to be made. Just as the Captains expressed, she was very worried about the fate of her people if this war dragged on. What would she become if all that she was were released in the service of her people? Would all of them remain her people? Would Llyncu and Human be sundered?

These dire thoughts were interrupted by the arrival of her Chosen. Talon entered her room and went to one knee beside the table. Mila vacated the room, locking the hatch from the inside on her way out. No one was allowed to interrupt the Queen in private audience with her Chosen.

Alone with Talon, her hair lifted and threaded its way into his loose curls. Talon had anticipated her need and had not thread his ribbons before arriving. There were serious discussions to come, but not this minute. The Queen's eyes began to glow and gave herself up to the pleasure of having so great a predator submissive to her will. She lost herself to touching the enigmatic mind, to manipulating his pleasure center until he trembled and groaned. Her coils worked beneath the neck of his tunic and caressed the muscled length of his torso and back.

There had been no time for such intimacy between them when she had not yet matured. Then she had to take up the reins of the kingdom. She would have this moment, however, this beginning. Talon' short coils curled around her own offering his unwavering loyalty and support. She was all he had, all he wanted and this moment was only the start of his reward for dedicating his life to her. His body swayed and he was pinned to the board of her dominance and pleasure at his submission. She could do with him as she wished and he would revel in it. He belonged to her, for always.

For the first time BrightLance let her control slip and touched his mind and body with intent to test his limits.

Sensations rushed throughout his body which Talon had not experienced. His trembled, yet remained in control, still determined to be. The Queen felt the first stirrings of the predator demanding to be fulfilled. She would have his pleasure at her command. Coils barely stroked across his skin, some massaged and others restrained him. His tunic was stripped away. Pleasure pain electrified his nerves and Talon gasping, began to struggle. His upper body eventually collapsed against her hip. His body contorted in its efforts to escape the new intensity. Her coils were a constricting, stinging blanket when his body arched. Muscles bunched and spasmed with the most fierce orgasm of his entire twenty eight summers.

BrightLance caressed him as he shook and gasped for breath. She sighed in contentment and reveled in his pliant, sweat soaked body bound by her coils. For the first time her coils transmitted the flavor of Talon' sweat and semen to her tongue. He had done well, fought hard not to lose control. She tortured him with pleasure through his mind and body. No one else could have withstood an attack on both fronts. She let him feel her approval that he had resisted. She wanted that as much as his submission. Now he was truly her Chosen. No one else could ever give him this. No Cadre or civilian or denizen of the Court would be able to divert him. After he had come to her, she had not demanded his purity. Yet he had maintained it for the sixteen summers he had been in the Cadre. A most wondrous gift. He was hers to torture, hers to pleasure, hers.

\*\*\*

Mustafa twisted his cloak's flapping edges into the belt at his waist. His blew scarf had to be wrapped again to conceal his face and keep out the bits of pine needle and grit. The debris cut when it struck unprotected skin. He shifted the backpack of vittles to sit easier on his shoulders. The winds were rising faster than anticipated, which meant the small party he was leading may have to hold up in the mountain passes for the night on their return from this bramble forest. He had every intention of leaving the food they carried in the caches before CatsEye flooded the forest gold. Mustafa worried about Fredric's rabble finding the supplies they secreted onto his lands. It happened more than the FreeSoul's wished, but it was better to keep attempting to provide than carry the knowledge that people were starving to death on your doorstep.

The shadows within the forest were suddenly deeper, and black began to swallow the faint trail the men followed. Unexpected green tinged clouds were writhing in the grip of a sudden rise in the relentless wind. Now they would be lucky to have CatsEye to see them home tonight. They would probably spend it wet and very cold. At least Mathru was not breeding this time of year. To walk unsuspecting into a knot in the dark. The thought made him shudder. Although Mustafa imagined there would be next to nothing next summer for the nasty pod creatures to feed on. Perhaps they would starve to death. The world certainly would be an easier place to live in without them.

Air rushing through the mountain and canyons behind them began a moan and bass drumming that would have frightened someone new to the environs. The five good Samaritans pressed on intent on their mission, making good time on the familiar route.

The group was very near the drop off point when a chill slithered up Mustafa's back and a sense of dread filled his heart. Panicked, the guide's hand waved his party back and away. He did not have to look to know the other men dropped to hug the ground. The sounds of their heavy breathing stilled abruptly. It was as if no one crouched at this back. Mustafa attempted to control his fear. Why was he so panicked? It would not do to run or make a move that would get someone hurt. He would not have been this frightened over wandering dearhart. Whatever was ahead meant them no good. He thought men would not have frightened him so. They could hide from men in this weather.

Fredric's so called soldiers had never killed anyone of the FreeSouls when raiding their relief caravans. The man was filled with madness, but not so much that he wanted to push one group of people he disdained into the arms of the demons he actually feared. There was much debate in the streets and cafes about what should be done now, however. Luc and Mano had been beaten very badly only a few days past, barely making it back, after the rabble harassed them to the borders for sport. Mano had yet to regain consciousness and his family was clamoring for justice.

Mustafa signaled for Powa to come to his side. The young man took orders well and would keep watch while he attempted to find out what had nearly given him heart failure. The food would serve no one returned to Stara. So even unnerved as he was, Mustafa could not see turning back unless a really big taguldal was out there. Taguldal feared nothing and no one except the demon's most talented magick users. They wrapped around you until your bones were crushed. Shaking off the chill that gripped him, Mustafa squeezed Powa's shoulder before easing away on his moccasined feet through the tangled brush. The hefty weight of his kilij was some comfort. If death was imminent he would at least go down fighting for his life against the beast.

Too late, too late! Mustafa did not need the light of CatsEye to see the wide coiled body rocking slightly as the great muscle constricted the bodies of an unknown number of men and horses and swallowed. Brush and new saplings were smashed flat in a wide break in the forest. He made every effort to move silently away hoping the strangled whinny of dying animals would cover his retreat. He had never imagined one so big. Unlike the old Earth cousin, taguldal was very aggressive and would chase prey dragging any thing they had already caught along with them. But this thing was huge!

Mustafa was shaking and damp with fear sweat by the time he got back to his men. He was simply blank with terror. It was so hard to think. He saw, it was just too terrible. He prayed none of the other caravans had . . .

Mustafa choked on bile and spasmed as silently as he could onto the ground. Powa gave him water to rinse his mouth.

The men were frightened by his reaction, but they kept quiet. He was the most experienced here. If he was like this, it had to be horrific. They could backtrack and circle around whatever the danger was. They may still reach the cache before dawning.

Mustafa was considering. It had to be Fredric's men. Surely he would send out another party when they did not return. He did not want to make contact with them. Yet Mustafa hated to waste food. No FreeSoul would participate in such a sacrilege. They must try to leave the food for those in need.

Rain began to beat them in steadily decreasing temperature. The men continued on their way, soaked but determined.

\*\*\*

Casper kept a wary eye on the dark figures crouching in the rain beneath the bulk of the irritated Pegasors. The beast did not like water. They hissed and growled while the wind driven drops rolled off their feathered hides. The woman never took her eyes from him. She seemed to have no problem holding the position, but was obviously not happy about being here. The young man called her Reaper. Their Cadre braids was thick with ribbons and Casper imagined their hair was soaked in blood. You certainly did not have the name of death himself if it was not earned. That was the Cadre way, even the FreeSouls knew that much about them.

He never thought he would see a day when FreeSoul's would be beholding to such as they. But Emrah was alive and may just survive his injuries. Was Allah not merciful when He lead the young man from a torturous death in Haven's blighted forest? The one called Scout had spied him even amid the thick foliage of the forest and dared Haven's land to rescue him. Casper tried not to stare. If they were not in armor, they would not attract much attention, he thought. Brown hair, brown eyes, so ordinary looking, except for the fierce beasts gnawing at their armored shoulders and snuffling their hair.

Healer Kameko scrubbed up. She had only stopped at the outpost to inoculate the men with the flu preventative they needed to stay healthy during their rotation on the border. The harsh weather was setting in early again this season. She did not expect to perform emergency surgery to keep one of their Samaritans alive. Caregiver Natane assisted her, by tucking her unruly white curls under the surgical cap and tying it off. One of the guards would assist the Caregiver in scrubbing up before they both went in to stitch together poor Emrah.

Word had gone out to Stara of the attack and rescue. The Senators were hysterical over Cadre being on their side of the border rather than the murder of the Samaritans and the blessed return of Emrah to his family. Honestly most of the Senators were too old to be wagging about ruling over anyone. Younger minds and able bodies should be sitting in those seats as far as Kameko was concerned. Wisdom was only available in the elders for a short time after their winters set in. Once proved deteriorating, the old guard should step down.

There were too few women in those seats for one thing. The Healer believed that her gender would be more likely to take a harder line with these Haven brigands. It was their sons and husbands going out to take food to people who had laid down and let some hate filled spew destroy their lives. Even now her coalition of female professionals was lobbying for more seats to be opened to other families of the mountains. Kameko may be a physician, but as far as she was concerned pacifism only worked during times of peace and there had been few peaceful days since Fredric's last efforts to 'conquer' Daear.

She could not hold back the chuckle that erupted into complete laughter at the thought of Haven ever getting through the passes or up the great Gates to the Queen's Palace. A quick glance at the black armored duo brought her back to the effort to close Emrah's wounds. He had taken more than one sword stroke and broken an arm during the run for his life. The biggest danger was from blood lose.

From what he managed to tell his rescuers there had been none of the usual warning. They had been spotted, were quickly surrounded, the food and medicine taken. They did not draw their swords as FreeSoul's only believed in defending themselves from the poisonous world. There fellow man must be met in peace.

The Samaritans were charged by the horses and cut down without mercy.

As the healers moved into the room, Reaper and Scout remained outside, one eye on the wary FreeSoul guardians and an ear for any unusual activity in the room where the women worked to patch up the young man they had discovered. Scout had not hesitated to push his Pegasor into Haven's territory when he spotted the staggering figure before it collapsed at the forest edge. His reputation would leap again, for CatsEye and the sun were obscured and the wind treacherous when he insisted someone was hurt over Reaper's skepticism.

Blood drew predators and he was damned if he intended to fight some monstrosity while they paraded up and down the borders. Oddly enough it appeared a tagudal had interrupted the brigands attack but not before the other Samaritans had been killed. Fredric's men fled, being chased by the biggest taguldal ever described. Reaper was sure shock had addled the boy's mind. Taguldal never reached such dimensions she insisted. Scout could care less, if it ate Fredric's men.

The rain fell heavier. The Pegasors roared in annoyance, startling the dark bearded fellow that watched them from the doorway. Reaper graced the nervous guard with laughter. This did not reassure the other FreeSouls guarding the trail up to the outpost overlooking the pass and the forest.

\*\*\*

Fredric Brooks paced. He grit his teeth. He smacked his closed fist against his thigh repeatedly. The goblet of recently distilled liquor had cracked against the wall leaving a puddle. The room reeked of the raw fermented swill his men insisted was ale. He wanted to know why his nephew Roddy had not returned from his patrol. Mason had finally taken a group into the forest to track him down. Roddy had better not be siphoning off the supplies for his own ends. Fredric would address his betrayal in the public square and execute him with his own hands. The people would understand and appreciate their leader's sense of justice. All of Haven's people were equal under the law. Fredric would have justice. He paced. He raked his sweaty palms through his greying blonde hair. He paced. Rain began drumming on the roof tiles. He paced.

Mason Brooks was no fool. He had not been the favored son just because he was born first. He was the smart one, the one they could not beat. Kacey and Luthor were dead. One in a drunken fight with one of the rabble they called an army and the other during the last battle with Daear. When Roddy did not return, Mason figured he had met with ill fortune. Considering this was Nadredd, ill was a way of life. Fredric's grandiose dreams were dead like their people. His great grandfather had turned the people from survival of Nadredd to believing they were owed. The learned ones had slowly been conscripted over the rotations until most of what his father called peasants could barely read and write. But most of those were dead now anyway or scattered on the winds.

Barter was life's blood on Nadredd. So with barren fields where there should be crops, and every hand turned against them, Fredric's grand army would be starving before winters end.

Scavengers hid in the wilderness all along the borders of Daear and the FreeSoul's mountain passes, attempting to prey on anyone who could provide sustenance. Regrettably there were very few of those as his men raided the bold FreeSouls who attempted to bring sustenance.

The forest was no place for man nor beast with winter coming on early, again, and little prey to be had. Dearhart were scarce. Last winter there was plenty of meat, if nothing else. The garrison was still overflowing with indolent wastrels. When Haven rode against Daear, Mason noticed that a number of them were conspicuously absent. Supposedly off discussing tactics or protecting the rear. He killed a few just to get his point over. Now he was expected to strip the land of the little of nothing left to feed the scum another winter in hopes of another summer offensive.

He did not wish to think about the welcome he would receive when he arrived on his sister's doorstep seeking a share of her dwindling supplies for their father.

Ten dawnings past, a patrol sent some FreeSoul Samaritans back through the pass beaten within an inch of their lives. Mason had been livid. If the pacifists took up the sword with Daear, they could very well over run Haven. Beside their scum, Fredric had no more 'peasants' to send to the sword. His father scoffed at the idea, but Mason knew the FreeSouls studied hand to hand fighting and practiced with their swords. They had taken oaths to never use those skills against other intelligent life, but if enough of their people were slaughtered that vow would be worthless.

It was well known that many of the FreeSouls felt like Fredric did about the demons of Daear.

Information had come their way by a stray messenger bird now and then. His father laughed at the occasional betrayal of their own and joked about making sure he got rid of them too, after the demons were disposed of. What made them think they were pure humans? What a ridiculous notion.

Unlike Fredric, the FreeSouls did not want to fight with the demons directly and waste their lives over ancient history. Collectively they believed war was illogical when diplomacy offered peaceful solutions to disagreements. With lucrative trade and free access to all the land beyond the mountains Daear and Stara managed to support their separate populations and thrive.

Mason had come very late to the awareness that this was a losing battle. After rotations of the rhetoric and conditioning, it took that last battle to drive home the utter futility of this effort. The King had been killed by a perfect subterfuge, but all of Mason's best fighters died in the effort. Instead of becoming dispirited Daear's soldiers had rallied behind a screaming beanpole of a witch who killed everyone she could catch. Demons turned up in the middle of his fighters and laughed while they killed effortlessly, as if harvesting grain on a summer dawn. They had no fear. They were demons.

When his father had sent Farrell off to be slain and instigate more bloodshed, Mason had been speechless. But then he had never stood in the way of that boy being kicked around. Knocking him about with his own fist to keep up appearances was easy. Father had been literally foaming at the mouth when word leaked back that Farrell and his Chosen was alive and under the care of the demon Queen. No one had seen him, but purloined copies of the FreeSoul ambassador's dispatches had revealed he was surrounded by Cadre in some secret place where no one walked unless they courted immediate death.

Gathering his scattered thoughts, Mason refocused on his task as his company rode into dark forest. It would be a lot less unpleasant if the rain would cease and the sun or CatsEye was lighting the way. Fredric thought Roddy was betraying him. But then, he thought that of everyone these days. Roddy was simply too lazy for the effort. He took to killing but not to planning and sneaking about.

Mason unsheathed his sword, already wary that the forest was so still. Even with the rainfall there should be rustling in the brush as some of the less dangerous serpents took cover. There was no sense of life at all. He directed two of his men to scout around for sign and pushed deeper into the gloom.

\*\*\*

Cherish was at a loss. She knew father would welcome the death of her obstinate husband, but Eustace did not die, though it was expected. Medicines that might be the difference between life and death for their retainers at some future date, were being used to treat his mortal wounds. He was in pain, but he would not die. Wringing her chapped hands, Cherish paced the length of the hall, considering her options. Eustace had requested she end his painful existence with an excess of sleeping draught. He was exhausted and wanted the torture to end. But, if he died father would send those horrible animals to take up space in this hall and probably hand her off to one of them. Her heart began to race with panic. Her palms sweat and dampened the faded blue of her skirt as she twisted it in her hands. What to do? What to do?

Cherish was the last child of Kate, and though her father disparaged the birth of a daughter, his other five sons allowed him to pretty much ignore her existence until she turned sixteen summers. Despite protests from his wife, she was handed over to Eustace and told she was married. She had lived on the estate ever since. Taking to the task she had been trained for, running the household and going to his bed.

She could read and write a little bit, but her expertise was making the supplies they had last through the severe winters. It had become harder and harder to do so. Now she

worried because the stands of forests near their estate were bare
of dearhart and there were more serpents than ever. Her men
recently set a fire to eliminate some of the rising population. It
seemed to have worked to drive them out, but the dearhart did
not return to the surrounding area.

Cherish sent some of the workers out to bring food in
from the FreeSoul's caches. It was very dangerous because if
her father discovered them it was a death sentence for treason.
She was sheltering people and their children also. He would be
furious about that. It added to her dilemma. Fredric preached
and swore and ranted. She had yet to see any benefit for
herself and certainly not for the family, with one brother in
the hands of demons and two dead. After her little brother was
born there was only violence in her life. She was exhausted and
frightened and despaired of it. She only wanted to run away.
The room seemed to tilt and she swayed to one side. Run
away, run away, run.

Hours had passed while the distraught soul sat at the hall
table clutching her prematurely greying hair and shuddering.
She had waved away her servants and spoke to no one. The
idea to just leave. Abandon the children? No she just could
not do so, not the defenseless children. Farrell's image rose in
her mind. She had never seen his face, only the top of his
shorn head and an occasional glimpse of his tiny bruised body.
It had been too frightful to sneak him any food or attempt to
speak to him. She learned quickly that he was punished
severely if anyone thought he was using his demon powers.
Cherish had never seen any powers and only heard tales of the
demons. What if it was a lie? What if her father was insane?
Why would her brothers let him do these things?

The world outside the hall was black. Rain slashed in icy waves against the walls. She would tend her husband this night. Rouse him, make him understand and hope he could stay conscious enough to speak to his surviving men at arms. If she listened in she would know who to trust. An over dose of the sleeping draught could be used for more than Eustace if necessary. She would gather the people who were as desperate as she. They would risk the forest and the mountain passes. Whatever father thought of the mixed races of the FreeSouls, Cherish knew the most important thing. They would take in her people. They would not turn the children away.

\*\*\*

Cleatus fumed. He was so damned mad he could barely see straight. Not a good way to be on watch duty below the gates of the demons. He felt his face heat again recalling how Brandy goaded him until he took a swing at the idiot. Of course he did not come close to hitting the bastard. So Colby had to throw in his jeering comments. When Cleatus thought he would burst he was so mad, dear brother sent him off to watch for demons. Their laughter and snide remarks followed him over the sounds of pelting rain and wind.

The demons knew they were here. The guards behind those old ship's doors could sometimes be seen looking down the mountainside. They must laugh themselves sick at the pack of fools scurrying around in the forest like llyncas during a swarm. There was no way up that mountain passed the llygred even after dark. The damn things crunched underfoot and stank. During the day even a blind man could see anyone attempting the climb. Another damn stupid idea of father's!

Cleatus had been here since the last battle. Field operations his father called it. Damn waste of time it was. He was shivering and fevered and too damned wet with no end in sight. Had that been known, Colby might be tempted to end him for good. His twin had never been pleased to have responsibility for overseeing his training. Training, another joke at his expense. Colby's strategy meant beating Cleatus until he had to fight back or die. Cleatus was considered the younger son and knew his size was the reason the family decided he was weak in comparison to his brothers. Even Cherish was a head taller, at least when he saw her last.

It had been many seasons. Father had Eustace come to visit often, but Cherish was left behind. Mother had gone into seclusion after Cherish was married off. Frankly he was not sure Fredric had not killed her too. Would not surprise him. Whenever father was preaching about the evils of demons and taking back what was theirs, Cleatus was hard pressed not to ask why they waited so long. He was not stupid. This winter was coming earlier than the last. Last winter there were next to nothing harvested before the bad weather. This season there was no one left to do the work and the weather had turned the very next dawnings after the battle. All he remembered of that day was waking up in his bed covered in blood and stuck to the blew he slept on.

As his fever rose, he pushed the sodden tattered cloak away from his damp body. The chill air and water was a relief for the moment. He knew he would be wrapping up tight when the shivering started again. At this point in his misery, even the halls of Haven would be welcome and his bed. He would give all of his inheritance for a bed right now. Damn demons, damn father!

\*\*\*

Pandrau watched the men she selected for their foray into the forest assemble at the gate. They were dressed in tanned dearhart and moccasins. Blades were strapped to thighs and the inside of wrists. The hilts of short swords could be seen over their shoulders A few of the men had fought at the front, which many of the Palace guards had not done before. When the Queen had expressed the desire to remove the rabble lurking about, Pandrau had asked for the chance to go and do it. She was bored and her guards would suffer for it. Complacency was not allowed.

If the day their enemies ever got too close, she would no longer let it be said that all that stood between their Queen and death was the Cadre. In her heart it infuriated her that the citizens were singing ballads of the Cadres bravery and the death of MeekBlade. The bravery of BrightLance was no question, but her guards, Pandrau's guards were brave and skilled and willing to die for their Queen as much as any Cadre.

Colby rolled over and scowled at the lumps that lay about him. Useless scum, but at least they had to hunt and bring in game to eat. He thought they may be better off than the fools remaining in the estate. Yes he was cold, and wet, but his belly was full. He was not going to bed hungry. He imagined even Mason was tightening his belt with short rations these day. Colby snorted. Oh wise brother stalking around spouting all that rot that father spewed. The General of father's army. What an enormous joke.

Here in the forest below Daear, Colby had a full belly every night. He would probably make it through the winter and then before spring slammed the plains with rain, he would return home with the sad news of a renewed assault of demons which devastated his few loyal men while the rest deserted him. Father would foam and spew, but probably kill a few of the cowards that sucked off their table and go back to planning his great war and liberate them all from the demons. Good Luck with that!

Paquin crouched in the brush watching the deeper shadows where wheezy gasps could be heard. Whoever they were, it was bad. Sick he thought and maybe unconscious. It would not due to move to quickly and get himself killed. Pandrau would never let him forget it. He pressed the small tracker at his waist so she would come to him and settled into wait. The others were slipping passed him deeper into the woods. He felt her first. Pandrau's coils slipped into his hair. In a moment she sent him on and moved closer to the trembling boy beneath the trees. A youth, very ill. She could feel the heat from where she crouched before him. He was burning up. She moved. Cleatus sprang up, blade flashing. He charged, slashing at whatever had come up on him in the dark. Terror spurred his actions. He could not see it.

Past rotations avoiding fists and kicks, had him ducking the unseen thing and slashing continuously to make contact and kill whatever it was. Pandrau felt like a fool as she ducked and blocked the rain of blows. He was a fierce fighter with more than a little knowledge of hand to hand. He blocked as many of her attempts to bring him down without killing him and that knife had already nicked her twice. How embarrassing. Pandrau rolled, to come in low and barrel him down. Her coils encircled his knife welding arm as her blade slipped between his ribs. Cleatus went slack in shock and pain. He wanted to scream, but there was no breath. He wanted to yell to cry, but there was no breath.

Breath, oh please, he needed to breath!

He managed one fretful whimper.

Pandrau felt the life leave the feverish body and for a moment felt the regret that this mere boy had to lose his life. She had wanted to spare him, find out who he was and what he knew about Fredric and his pseudo army. But it was too late now. He was determined to fight and she could not spare more time. She needed to ask BareBlade to train her if it took her this long to take down an ill youth. Pandrau allowed herself another moment of regret, then faded into the forest, cleaning her blade against her thigh. It was a given she would have no more soft hearted moments this night.

Paquin signaled the other guards he was coming in and got a response. He did not want anyone to kill him by accident. His heart was still beating at an accelerated rhythm. Part of him hoped he would not have to kill anyone, however to go home without drawing blood would mean he failed in his duty to the Queen.

It was not long before the tracker lead him to Jovan and he felt a little better not being alone on this venture. Jovan slipped his hand in Paquin's. His fingers moved quickly in the sign language they were all taught to use when any sound would be dangerous. Jovan advised him that the camp had been discovered and at least ten men slept, oblivious to their presence. They moved together, the trackers giving them the location of their other companions. The intent was to capture for information. As one the guards converged on the slumbering forms. Heavy hilts of short blades smacked into heads more than once. A quick injection of a deeper sedative and these fools would wake up in BareBlade's cells.

Whatever it was, Colby could not hear it now. He was suddenly wide awake without a clue as to why. The men were sleeping soundly and knowing his stupid brother, he was sleeping as well while some coiling menace nestled right next to him before having him for breakfast.

Colby snorted, and just like that he knew the world had gone to shit. He came up from his cloak with a shout to the men, swinging his sword. It met steel with twang and spark and Colby found himself sorely pressed. He shouted once more for the men and realized he was abandoned by the cowardly bastards. He roared in anger slashing wildly. Then charged his opponent swinging his cloak at them. There was a startled exclamation and he followed through with a thrust that stabbed whoever was fighting him. They went down with a yelp, but he tripped over them in the dark when they began struggling upright. The fellow grunted in pain and wrestled to get away from him. Colby cursed in breathless gasps while he struggled to stab his assailant. Then there was a flash of light and Colby thought CatsEye had never been that bright. He knew no more.

Damn damn damn, it hurt. Jovan grit his teeth, but could not stop the tears that overflowed. Since he was wet and it was dark no one would know. The scum had skewered him on that damn sword and then had nerve to fall on him. Jovan was struggling to fight the smelly hulk off when suddenly he was smothering. Jovan did not know who pulled the unconscious muskie off, but he was damned grateful as he gulped in icy and very fresh air. He would not remember passing out.

The jokers he worked with would never tell who pulled big muskie off of him.

\*\*\*

Mustafa reasoned they were far enough north to safely turn back to the mountains. He was sore at heart over their failure. Every time he moved east or south, the dread would return in full force. North or west left him nothing but his disappointment that the food they carried would be wasted. For three days they had walked, not daring to stop longer than to shift their packs a little easier on their shoulders.

It was raining again. The only relief was the thicker forest kept some of the water away. They were all cold. Thankfully there was some light to see by, though it remained very cloudy.

The thing he saw in the shadows of the trees would haunt his nightmares. He realized that more important than leaving food for people who may have already been food for that beast, he had to get his men home alive. So they pushed on north, prayed they weren't being tracked and hoped maybe they would find someone to pass off the foodstuffs to. They had come across two caches with untouched food. The most discussion they dared was disconcerted looks. They were dogged by depression and fear now.

A distant shout made them drop to the ground waiting to discover from what direction new danger was coming. Mustafa had kept them off the well-traveled paths up until now. This was a fairly clear stretch of forest so they would not have to creep along attempting to avoid causing any attracting disturbance. The really frightening thing was there had been nothing to disturb. All evidence pointed to abandoned borrows. No hawks flew over on their way to hunt during the cloudy days and not one coiled horror had been seen for the three days. There was no sign that the tagudal had been in this forest. Perhaps the snakes knew it was coming and crawled away.

Now they waited and prayed the beast had not been tracking them and caught some unsuspecting soul in its maw. His stomach roiled at the thought. They would not be able to help. Mustafa honestly believed it would take a near army of men to bring such a creature down. Warning must be sent to all. There was more shouting. There was too much noise, whatever the reason. That thing could be moving closer as foolish men voices grew strident.

There was nothing for it. Enemies or not they needed to be warned. Mustafa slipped the pack from his shoulders. He felt Powa and Sharad's restraining hands. He lowered the scarf of his turban and gave them a wan smile and a nod to reassure them. No, he did not want to be killed. Honestly he could wish the people of Haven had all gone into the wastelands far beyond these borders. The world would have continued with the most danger coming from long winded debates in the Senate meetings.

He pointed west. They should start without him. There

was nothing to debate and he was not to be moved by threats or cajoling, even silent ones. He wanted to get them away and yes he was tired. Desperately in need of his wife's best dishes spread out before him. He needed to hear his children laughing. He wanted back to the mountains. Mustafa pushed them off with an exaggerated sigh and stood, arms akimbo, until they moved out of sight.

He moved south and east toward the sounds of increasing disagreement. It was easy to slip closer to the careless men debating whether to turn back or continue their search. Mustafa observed them long enough to determine the leader. He was the silent one, grim, and shoulders squared with resolve. This one would not go back. He would probably kill one or two before he would allow that. Mustafa was able to drift around through the snarled brush and slip very close. He did not want this man to lash out and kill him, but he had to hear the message.

"I bring news."

Mason wheeled his mount to face the direction that soft voice had come from. The fools ceased their argument as his actions. Fear held them silent. Was Mason going to attack them? Something nasty lurked in these woods and they wanted back to the estate. There had been no sign of the errant cousin. It was damned foolish to keep riding about looking for the twit. He had probably run off.

"Show yourself. What news you bastard! Come out!"

Mason spurred his horse aggressively forward.

"I mean no harm to you or your men."

Mustafa stepped from beneath the thick boughs of the old pine. In its shadow he was barely revealed, a darker silhouette amid the branches.

"There is tagudal in these woods. I came upon it feeding. Sign suggests a group of men and horses were attacked. It . . . I tell you no lie I have never seen one so large. It will take more weapons and men than you have to kill it. There has been no sign of snakes or dearhart in these woods. I think they are fleeing north to escape it."

"Why should I believe you. This could be some trap!"

Mustafa took a deep breath and another step forward.

"Say what you will of us men of Haven, you know I will not raise hand against you. You know I gain nothing by coming to advise you of these events. This thing appears to have ranged far to the south. Our caches here are full of untouched food. No animals at all for the five dawnings I have been in these woods. Heed me and flee this place. Those you search for are dead. Even in this light my eyes did not deceive me."

Mason growled in rage. Dead. Roddy dead and the horses. Caches with food. He looked up to question the FreeSoul further, but found nothing but wind stirring the branches of the tree. Enraged he yelled for his men to beat the bush for the sneaky bastard. They needed the damned food.

Haven's men were crashing around making enough noise to raise the dead. Mustafa sat tight. His stomach was barely holding on to the rations he had consumed at dawning. It was a very near thing the non-believers had not killed him. The big one was so angry and the others so frightened, he had simply levered himself into the branches and they had not realized. Hopefully he could remain still long enough for them to move away. He would continue north for a ways and then turn toward the mountains. Mustafa was more determined than ever to get home.

No trace of the FreeSoul was discovered and the men were clamoring to return with the news of the tagudal. Mason had no desire to return to the estate and listen to his father's ravings. They had no Roddy, they had no food. The forest was empty of game. The pacifist bastard could not have been lying about everything. Tagudal. He shivered with revulsion. Nothing on Nadredd was as disgusting as those monsters. If it was big enough to take out Roddy's entire company it was a giant of a snake.

Mason brought his mount to a halt. He was short of breath and trembling. Exhaustion dropped on his shoulders like an anvil. What was he doing rampaging around the forest? This would bring the monster to his location. This was not finding game for the rabble to eat. He had been lost to his rage and resentment for too long. When he called the men rushed to his side. Their eyes were wide and white with terror, driven by their lurid imaginings. His command to return was barely leaving his lips before the men rushed away to the main trail. They never looked back. Cowards the lot.

# Sedition

Mason was the last of the dispirited band to ride through the gates of Haven.  The men rushed their mounts to the barns behind the house. He knew their panicked report would insure many empty places at the table tonight. Though where the fools could go, he had not one idea.

His heart swelled with contempt of the huddled crowd of Fredric's supporters. They still dressed warm yet were disgruntled over the lack of meat. Not one of the so called elite had lowered themselves to hunt for food. He was no one's servant. How dare they look at him demanding he provide. The idiots were fit for nothing less than practice dummies on the training field. He spat at the feet of one of the most corpulent and dismounted before the door of his home while the man blustered in outrage. For once the sight of an underfed servant held his eye as the boy rushed with lowered head to care for the exhausted horse. The hay racks were still full even if there was no grain. Though Mason wondered how long before mold would be a problem in the coming winter.

"What is this? Where is Roddy? What the hell are you doing back? Where is that fool?"

Mason ignored the tirade. He grabbed his father by the arm and practically dragged him through the hall to the private office near the back of the house.

"What the hell is the matter with you Mason? Have you gone mad? Get your . . . "

He was stuck speechless as his slighter body was pitched into the chair behind his desk. Mason loomed over him, filthy and red faced and screaming.

"Roddy is dead. His men are dead. There is no meat to be had in the forest. Tagudal rules there. A huge one, big enough to drive everything away. There is not one dearhart, one serpent or one of those coiled horrors hanging from the trees. There is no food old man. Do you hear me? There is no food to be had. The caches are full of spoiled food because no one is alive to empty them. We searched the forest for days. The damn Samaritans have disappeared. The forest is empty of anything living.

Do you hear old man? Do . . . you . . . hear . . . me?"

Fredric was pressed back into his seat by a screaming red faced stranger. For only a moment fear skittered about the older man's gut. Then, Fredric took a deep breath. His expression passed from surprise and fear to resolve.

"So you come in here screaming like a woman and expect what? Do you think I will pat you on the back and say oh poor baby?"

Mason was again left footed. He stared in consternation at this old man. Determination shown in Fredric's eyes. His chin lifted and the light of fanaticism lit his face like a beacon in the pitch.

The slap turned Mason's head sharply, compromising his balance. Shocked, he could not remember the last time his father struck him. He collapsed against the wall and leaned there struggling for control against rage and fear.

"Pull yourself together boy! You are becoming like that scum that scurries around our door, always whining. Where are your balls man? Where is the son I raised? Where is the general of my army? Hard times are upon us and you turn coward on me, you of all people?"

"I am no coward father. Well you know. I have killed more than you ever thought to put to the sword. I speak not from fear but from truth. You cannot feed these so called nobles of pure blood and the scum that waters their pants every time I say we must ride out. The forest are as clean as our courtyard. There is nothing father, nothing at all. Unless you expect us to feed this rabble pine nuts and branches."

Mason stare was still a bit crazed. Somewhere inside, swimming with all his other frustrations, was the fact the old man hit him. Resentment, ever present, began to fill him up. So he was of no more worth than these fools who hovered and flattered. No more worth than his brother who died fighting and was never acknowledged for that. No more worth than Cleatus and Farrell who were said to be unnatural for reasons Mason had never seen. He had never seen, only believed. Before rage could make Mason blind once more, Fredric spoke.

"Clean yourself up and get going to Eustace. Dying or not he owes us. Pick up the supplies he agreed to send and get back here. We can still recoup and take our place as masters over all these unnatural creatures. You must have patience Mason. Patience is the mark of a mature individual. When things look their worst that is when our blood will prove true. We will persevere. We will triumph in the end. You will see and then you will have to admit that your father had not steered you wrong. I will leave behind my legacy and, you my son, will be master of this world!"

Fredric had approached as he lectured and at the end grabbed his son by both shoulders and shook him in fond exasperation.

"Yes father. Yes, you are right. For, forgive me for doubting. I am, I am just tired of beating these cowards that serve us into shape. It seems a hopeless task."

Inexplicably Mason suddenly felt overcome with a real sense of utter failure. His entire life had been spent believing his father had the right of it. Now here he was after thirty five summers, standing in his father's office feeling like an overwhelmed little boy.

Squaring his shoulders Mason shook off his father's grasp.

"Thank you for reminding me all is not lost. I will not lose faith again father. I promise."

He met his father's eyes with a smile stretching his mouth.

Fredric laughed and clapped his son solidly on the back.

"There now boy. All you needed was a little reminder of what we are fighting for. You have the right of it. Never lose faith. You will see it all will pay off in the end. Now, now no more of this downcast attitude. Off you go. Eustace maybe a little reluctant to part with his share, but be sure to remind him of the consequences if you need to. Take what men you may need to haul the goods. Bring me word back if Cherish has gotten herself pregnant yet. I am telling you that girl is proving she is more like her mother every day. It is a woman's place to bear the fighting men. Perhaps Eustace is less of a man than he seemed."

The door closing behind Mason went unnoticed during Fredric's vocal concerns about Cherish and her inability to provide grandchildren for the great cause. In a state he would never be able to describe, Mason made it to his bedroom on the second floor and stripped off his filthy clothes. Hot water was already waiting. The servant girl shied away from him like always and hurried from the room. She had laid out his clothes. He could not remember when he last had a woman. Mason scowled at the thought of taking some frightened female to his bed. Father said it was their right and slept where he willed, unwilling or not. Men protesting died. If they did not protest, they were cowards. His father was insane.

Mason sat in the water until it cooled. Josef entered the room, bowed and waited to empty the dirty water. Mason knew he was standing naked and staring overlong at the older man.

"Josef, I have a task for you. The most important task of your life. Sit here and pay close attention."

Josef allowed himself to sit at the very edge of Mason's bed. He kept a wary eye as the young man toweled himself off. Gradually Josef's eyes grew wider and wider still. Eventually his mouth hung open. He believed he was dreaming as words continued to flow from the mouth of this man he had loathed his entire life. Josef and Mason shared a birth date, but you could not have guessed by sight. Josef was stoop shouldered and thin. Dark shadows and gaunt features made him appear well into his winter rotations. He was trembling when ordered to get up from the bed.

"This is not for me understand. If there is anyone here you care about do what I say. There is little time. If, if my mother is still alive, plead with her to flee this place with you. But do not delay. Anyone who will not go may well be food for the tagudal. I must go and see if my sister still lives and take her to the FreeSouls. They will at least take care of you all since you have no training with weapons and you have children. Go quickly Josef otherwise some of the scum will steal the horses and run off. You will be helpless if that happens."

He handed over the little pouch of pydru into the trembling hands of his manservant.

"I know you do not wish to do this thing. But I am one man and I cannot kill all of them. Just one pinch with the sleeping draught in their dinner stew and they will be too ill this dawn to run off. An extra pinch and they will not awaken at all. It is your choice. But be gone before dawn whatever you decide. If you leave any horses they will come after you to steal what food you have. I will see my father distracted."

He turned his back to the man to dress and gave him no further mind. Josef had the chance to save his family and the other servants. If they were smart the word would spread to those who wanted out. Mason did not believe any of them would report this to Fredric or any of the other 'lords'. It was every man for himself and the demons take the rest. He ate the coarse bread and dish of cold stew he had ignored when he came in.

He paid little attention to damp skin as he dressed in long johns and his personal vest, beneath his heaviest sweater. He exchanged the indoor slacks for the heavier muskie lined leathers and stomped into his boots. He packed a saddlebag with tightly rolled change of clothes and extra blew. Then he cleared his weapons cabinet, secreting small knives on his person and strapping his short sword to his waist. He carried his hunting bow and supply of arrows over his shoulders before he left the room.

Mason's arrival in the kitchens caused a stir, but he did not hesitate going through the cupboards and shoving two loaves of hard bread in his saddlebag. He snared a canteen off the wall by the rear door and filled it from the pump. He never acknowledged anyone as he went about his tasks. He walked out without a word to advise his father he was leaving for Eustace estate as ordered. A grim twitch of his lips was the only indication he saw the sacks of vittles piled up near the rear door. The hot stew that would be carried over to the men's barracks was covered and waiting on the table. It took two men to haul that cauldron there and back three times a day. Soldiers should not have to fetch and carry their own food since they were risking death for a noble cause. Just more nonsense his father spouted and he, a blind fool, had believed every word.

Mason had nothing but a dim memory of a gentle woman he had not seen in rotations. He had nothing but Cherish's looks of fear and disdain. He had nothing but the bruised and battered faces of his younger brothers as the rotations dragged by and they were never strong enough, never smart enough always wanting. And, he remembered the day he had beat and kicked an underfed tiny little boy who shared his blood. The cries of that blond boy had not been given a thought in all these long rotations. Now Mason remembered every single plea. Please please please no no no . . .

Fredric acknowledged the knock on his office door with a grunt. He looked up to see his fresh washed son, outfitted for his journey, in the doorway.

"The rain has stopped. If you keep to the open plains you should be there before morning and back here before nightfall."

Mason made no comment about riding out in the pitch or the futility of getting anything from Eustace. He just stalked across the room and poured some of the ale they distilled here into two tankards. He would never drink this buckwheat piss again. He turned to his father and saluted him before handing him one of the tankards.

"A toast father to my renewed resolve. As I was bathing it came to me that you are right. Why should I take the word of any man who spins such tales and dares not lift a weapon in his own defense. I feel like a fool."

"Be at ease son. Doubts are the burden of a man, but we must hold true to our ideals. If we do not, lesser beings would attempt to overcome us. See how the demons wage war against us with unnatural creatures in their armies? True men should be allowed to live free and acknowledge their betters without the curse of this natural world tainting our existence. We will win through Mason. We will win through."

He dipped the cup back and swallowed.    One day

Fredric reassured himself, one day.

Mason gave a curt nod in return and emptied his cup. It would warm him for a minute if nothing else.

"Father if Eustace has died. Do you wish Cherish returned home?"

"Ah yes, well if he has died she will need a new husband. I have been giving it some thought.

We will send a few of the men next time so she can pick. Only send the most loyal Mason. Cherish has a soft heart, but she needs a man who will take charge of the estate and be loyal to me. Besides she needs babies to keep her busy until we can bring them into training. Do not speak of it for now."

"As you will it father. I should go while the weather holds. See you tomorrow night."

"Yes, yes. Go quickly." Fredric went back to the maps and charts on his desk planning. Always plans, plans and more plans.

When Mason entered the stables he went straight to the big brute at the rear. As dark as the pitch outside, Fredric had personally bred the stallion for the day he would march in triumph into the streets of Daear. Tonight he would take Mason away from here and neither of them would return.

If he died on the plains or fighting the demons Mason could accept that. To be eaten by a slimy monstrosity, no. If any of the FreeSouls are the bloody praised Cadre went after the creature then he would put his body and sword in their hands. If they allowed and had not killed him first.

"Boy, what do they call you?"

"I am Daniel, sire."

"Stop with the sire. If you had food and your father was

a insane killer, you would be me. When I die my blood will spill as red as your own. Take one of the heavier mounts and saddle it. Grab whatever blew or cloak you got. You are coming with me. Josef will be moving slower with his people. They may travel north anyway. I did not want to know what he would do other than leave. We ride south to Eustace estate to get my sister. If you want the FreeSouls may take you or the Rovers. I just know I can get you there if you want to live."

Daniel said nothing, although his wide grey eyes spoke volumes. He hurried to the sorrel that he had pretty much raised and threw blew and saddle on quickly. He ran and climbed the ladder to the loft and dug his sweater and cloak out of the hay. The sweater had been tossed in a bin after llyncas had got to it. He picked off the slimy little larvae and watched them die in a pool of horse piss behind the barn. He had to wash the sweater three times before he could wear it. He slipped the knife he pilfered into his boots. No one wanted the thing as the tip was snapped off. Did not matter to him it was still sharp. The last thing was the heel of stale bread he had been hoarding.

Mason kept an ear out for anyone coming his way and disrupting his plans. He was aware of the arguments going quiet in the barracks after hot food arrived. Soon those men would be dead, or stinking the place up and wishing they were.

When he climbed into the saddle, Brute reared up and pawed the air. The boy had already wrapped his legs to protect him from coils because Fredric demanded it a constant. But at this point they might not even run in to any. Mason did not look back as he walked the horse from the barn. Daniel followed, the sorrel tossing his head about, enjoying being out even if it was dark and cold. The boy asked no questions, but moved quickly when ordered. He never got that kind of compliance from the scum army without fear of his fist and the edge of his blades.

Once they left the estate walls, Mason intended to attach a lead to the other horse if the weather went wrong. He had traveled so often to Eustace's estate he could find his way easily even in the pitch. He turned away from the rough road to the forest trails and headed further east before turning and going at a fast mile eating canter across the empty plain. Daniel settled into the saddle and fought to keep the big smile on his face from giving way to explosive laughter.

Josef slipped inside the Fredric's office. Their master lay sprawled across his maps and charts. Josef did not think Mason could kill him. A gargled snore confirmed it. Something stopped every man from killing a parent, unless they were a true monster he supposed. The great leader of men was drooling on his plans. Josef backed out of the room. The house servants had all packed what foodstuffs that would not spoil and rushed to gather their families. Josef really needed to blow his nose, but there was no time. He rushed from the house to the barn. He would not look where most of those men would wake up deadly ill in the morning. He would not look at the barracks, where some would be dead in their beds because their bodies were weaker and pydru was unpredictable at best. He did not want to think what Mason had originally planned for that small bag.

The barn doors swung open and Josef's sons rolled the hay wagon out into the courtyard. It was pulled by the draft animals. The cattle's great horns would be formidable weapons if they were attacked on the way, but they would be much slower going. Too many of their people were weak and could not make the journey on foot or horse. The irony did not escape Josef that the animals were healthier than any one servant on the estate.

He was relieved to see the wheels were wrapped in rags and the axles greased before being pushed outside. Josef would follow Mason south toward the Eustace estate. He himself had been there before to get supplies the past season. If the tagudal was headed north and very close to this place, they needed to be as far away south as possible. He knew where the pass was into FreeSoul territory and he would dare take it. His sons drove the cattle forward and as they rolled along the courtyard, people slipped from the shadows. Some were lifted into the wagon. Others rushed into the barn and came out riding and trailing horses behind them with hastily wrapped hooves and fetlocks. Luck was with them. Most of the men had not appeared for guard duty. It was easy to dispatch the nervous duo that did show up. At the courtyard gate the wagon stopped and more people rushed out and climbed in. In all he thought he had almost thirty people, counting a surprising number of teens and children. They were orphaned and worked for a roof and what scraps got tossed their way.

Josef recalled the days when everyone believed their destiny would be living in Daear, replacing the demons and ruling the planet. After much consideration he thought perhaps Nadredd rules everyone. Nothing that ever touched this cursed rock was ever the same. The people, the animals, the damn snakes. But as corrupt as the others were, they were not starving. They were not fleeing their only home in the night because monsters were coming to eat them. He had seen the demons on the battlefield, heard that awful joy filled laughter as blood rained around them. Never had he known fear such as that and he ran with the rest.

But now there was a tagudal, a giant one who ate men and horse all at once so the FreeSoul said. Mason had acknowledged those people had never been caught in a lie, even if some of them were foolish enough to think Fredric would honor any deals made to end the demons. Mason had said the man's voice was full of fear. Terror made a honest man of everyone. You knew at that moment if you were man or coward. In this Josef would gladly accept coward. He would flee and pray to whatever ruled this cursed land that the tagudal passed his poor deluded souls by.

Mason stopped on the rise and gaped at the dark edifice that should have been lit. Where were the guards on the walls? Where were the lights? He dismounted and hung the short sword and scabbard on to his saddle. He passed off the reins to the silent Daniel. When Mason pointed at his feet Daniel nodded quickly. Once again the man wondered why this untrained boy was able to obey orders like he had been a soldier all his life. It still amazed him. No use putting it off. He needed to slip down to the estate and discover where his sister was. If the tagudal had been here, there would be plenty of sign. He grit his teeth to quell rising nausea and move swiftly down to the gate.

There was no sounds except his own breathing and the stirring of the chill breeze. CatsEye illuminated the landscape for a moment. The wide gates of the estate stood open. They were not broken apart. It looked as if the entire household had departed. Mason slipped along the wall. He did not hear the snuffling of any animals. Eustace still had horses and a few cattle but they were not in evidence. Certainly the scent was too faint. Perhaps Cherish had abandoned the estate and fled to the FreeSouls on her own?

Mason eased into the dark house. He took a moment to orientate himself and proceed up the stairs to the second floor. He had never been up here before. Cautiously he felt along the wall and decided a lit candle or lamp would be of use. Maybe he could discover what happened. He did not want to think that there was men still out here that could have invaded the estate. If they had, they would have held the place for winter quarters not abandoned it. Mason realized he was panicked. The only decent thought that had ever crossed his mind may be to no purpose. Cherish could still be dead.

He fished his strike box out of his pants and got a spark on his first try. He disregarded the effort it took to steady the flame to catch the wick of the brace of candles. One by one the candles guttered and then the flame caught. Mason paid no mind to pictures on the wall or the worn rug he trod upon. The first door he opened had the look of his father's office. He took a look at the desk to see scribbled notes and much splattered ink. It looked like someone's crude effort to parcel out food stores.

He continued to look into doors he passed to find dusty unused bedrooms for guest or children that never arrived. It was when he opened the double doors at the end, the scent burst onto his senses. A body lay on the wide bed, clothed for sleep in gown and robe. It was Eustace with arms crossed over his chest, his face mottled in the first stages of decay. Mason did not linger. He made is way downstairs until he found the kitchen. It had been cleared of everything. Even the flour barrels were empty. Perhaps they had time to use it to take extra bread on their journey. Josef would have had no time for such as that.

Mason moved off the estate and returned to find Daniel astride, prepared to flee if necessary. He thought he might come to like this boy. They returned to shelter in one of the outbuildings for the remainder of the night. After he spent some time imagining all kinds of horrors, Mason drifted into his first sleep in days. Nightmares plagued him. Coils take him if he developed a conscience at this late stage in his life.

Cherish looked around her at the scorched earth and black ruined trees. Even the dirt seemed to be scorched for life, a deep black ash that was too heavy to stir much in the wind. She felt some regret, but there were no snakes and no mathru. Any pods would have burned. That could mean they would not breed again in the new growth forest for a few seasons. Fires were rare in the forests on Nadredd. Even lightening was the least of their worries compared to the windstorms. She prayed the forest would return, rather ashamed her desperation led to this devastation. Her people were damp and cold, but buried under all the blew and sharing body heat made that a minor distraction. The odor of burned snakes still lingered though, caustic and eye watering at times.

The night Eustace gave his men at arms instruction to flee with the women and children, Cherish and been terrified. He had only just spoken to Joseph and the others before falling into this deep and final sleep. She had wept as she ushered the men from the room. The sleeping draught had been strong. He would not wake at dawning.

Eustace had been kind to her all these rotations, his pretense of intense jealousy had shielded her from her father's badgering and condemnations. She would miss him, she realized. He had never been affectionate, but always displayed a distant courtesy. He had loved his first wife, rare though that was in her experience. He accepted her because to reject her as wife probably would have gotten him killed and all his people conscripted. As it was, he and his men had fought in that last battle. A large number remained to rot on open ground for predators to feed on. No one dared return to bury the dead when they feared Fredric would just come in and take over. Not that they had numbers to defend it.

She feared the men would flee or worse, report to her father. She could not expect clemency from Fredric. Even her brothers had become people to fear. Mason was a cold distant figure. He never seem to realize she was there at all. The others were nasty drinking horrors, that brutalized everyone they supposedly ruled over. Though Cleatus was treated horribly by them, he rejected her efforts to comfort him. He became an evil tempered child. Father had him disciplined more than once for abusing the horses. She suspected he would spend time with Farrell when he could sneak about. That could not have been good at all.

She nearly fainted with relief when Joseph came to her and spoke with such deference. They would take everything and do as Master ordered. If nothing else they could scratch out some type of life in the caves if the FreeSouls would allow them that until summer claimed the plains again. He was loath to lower himself to asking for such mercy, but understood the children had to survive. Perhaps one day a real leader would rise up and take back their world from the demons. Contrary to everything her father preached this man was showing her respect and treating her with care.

The men at arms had surprised her further by organizing the animals and making any repairs to the wagons so everyone would not have to walk. To not have to sneak around in fear left her almost giddy. The men scoured the estate for every scrap of material that would be of some use. Cherish had them empty all her cloth and blew stores for possible barter. Eustace previous wife had very expensive materials preserved for dresses she never got to have made. They should be able to trade for food if they took them.

The women used every kitchen on the estate to bake bread for the journey. Though there would not have been enough for winter, it should get them through the pass. All the dried meats she had stored for a lean winter ration was packed for the journey. No one knew what they would find on the other side, but to die slowly here was not an option. If nothing else the FreeSoul's might allow them to shelter the children in the pass until they could return home.

The men wanted to move quickly having no desire to fight against the demons weakened from hunger. They cleared a trail through the forest, during the days everyone else packed, cooked and gathered fodder for the animals. Cherish looked back once, to thank the husband she left asleep in his bed these past three dawnings.

***

Strike and Shadow sat astride their Pegasors. The rain was gone for the moment and the twins enjoyed the faded light of the sun breaking through the clouds. Their coils danced together twining and parting, stroking and teasing in the air around them. Sometimes a few would lift higher, seeking the scent of any enemy approaching. Their eyes glowed sparkling topaz in the dawn light. Their mutual joy was not just an internal experience.

Below them, on a wide ledge tucking into thick travelers stew and biscuits, sat QuickStep and Shatter. They giggled and snorted as they shared poor jokes. QuickStep rested against the side of her Pegasor as it slumbered. Shatter had been sent out when there had been increased hostilities against the FreeSouls. BareBlade did not want any of his Cadre short changed of support if things escalated. QuickStep would protect her Chosen and someone needed to watch her back, especially if there was serious contact. Raze, as was her inclination, prowled the smaller passes and hovered over the cliffs in the dark.

As a squire, Shatter had excelled in hand to hand combat training. He won his Pegasor by punching it in the nose when it snarled at him. It lost a tooth in that round. Shatter was so ashamed, he spent all the rotations since, pampering the creature like a baby to make up for it. Even now that big head lay across Shatter's lap. In between bites and sips of water, the man's big gnarled hands scratched and plucked, removing shed feathers before they knotted in the fur. The Pegasor rumbled in pleasure.

The trio had arrived in time to question some errant spy Raze had detained. The man knew little of Fredric's plans, but was hoping to hear about any Samaritans going out to deliver food. After the twins lent their expertise to the interrogation, which involved little more than walking in the room, word was sent back about the true situation on Fredric's estate. The man knew of gossip indicating Fredric's daughter, had an estate further south also full of hungry people and only a few healthy men at arms. Perhaps they would be going home soon after all. Starving men had no fight in them after a certain point.

Then messenger hawks flew in from the FreeSoul outpost guarding the entry to the pass. A giant tagudal was reported northeast of the pass. The first report was speculated on and disregarded by the FreeSouls. Surely the descriptions were exaggerated. The twins were more believing because in their world nothing was impossible. Did they not exist when natural order would have suggested humans were all dead long ago? Were their own parents not human?

Then just eight dawns later a second hawk arrived advising it was confirmed by a party of Samaritans who actually had a visual sighting. They believed it had taken at least five dawns to move away from its location and circle back to the pass. Animals had fled the forest before them which proved the creature was on the move. The first victim was still unable to be returned up the pass to Stara, but the second group of Samaritans had come and gone still shaken by their close call.

The team leader and his men stopped to rest and relate their misadventure over tea and breakfast with their fellows before they moved on. More Cadre members in attendance surprised them. Admittedly they were extremely unnerved by the twins. They had never seen an obvious demon before and were repelled, but could not keep their eyes averted at the unusual sight. The man and the young woman who attended them appeared very comfortable. The twins had sat, eagerness practically visible, their hair drifting around the woman. She did not have the face of a killer.

A report came in the following dawns, hesitant and cautiously worded permission was granted by the Senate for Cadre to cross the pass and bolster the guardians outposts near the border. The FreeSoul border guards were ill equipped to handle something so large and dangerous. Daear was put on alert and messenger birds went out to Rovers and Searchers of its existence. Although not immediately threatened, the possibility of tagudal growing so large would be a concern to all.

Raze had made the run east to drop off more Cadre blasters for the FreeSoul guardians to have access to. Reaper and Scout were comfortable enough as this outpost had the largest number of men since the forest and its denizens began at the bottom of the pass.

Queen BrightLance had offered Daear's weapon of choice against such creatures if it intruded on FreeSoul territory. Now everyone was awaiting the Senate's decision. It could mean more Cadre on their land to weld the weapon unless the creature turned its attention to Haven lands. The twins really wanted to go hunt this giant creature. They had killed small ones, no less dangerous as they hunted by heat and sound vibration. This would not be a pleasure hunt regrettably, as this monster was large enough to consume horses and men with ease. The Cadre would need the gun if that was true.

Even so their enthusiasm was infectious and their joy being out of doors, so QuickStep continued giggling and Shatter remained bemused and meditative.

Far above the cry of a messenger bird caused the Pegasors ears to perk up. The twins had already been watching it approach, noting it must have come from the outpost near the end of the pass. Curiosity had them twitching with impatience. The bird flew into the portal above their heads to deliver its message to the FreeSouls who monitored this station. QuickStep and Shatter cleaned up their mess in anticipation of action and stood next to their Pegasors ready to ride out. An irritated growl herald the approach of Raze and her Pegasor. The mare had a serpent in her mouth and was surely annoyed at having her snack interrupted.

Gravel rolled from beneath someone's feet as they climb down the steps from the camouflaged cave. Hai approached the odd twins cautiously. He stopped a few feet away avoiding their eyes.

The twins shared a glance and grinned. They would not frighten the little man. BareBlade would make them pay for too much for misbehavior with the FreeSouls. Avoiding being beaten bloody in a sparring match just made sense. Were they not beautiful and bruises would look horrid? They exchanged a glance and grinned wider. BareBlade would make them work very hard for it too.

"Sirs, a dispatch from the forward outpost. The daughter of the mad Fredric has arrived and ask permission to shelter in the pass, or be permitted to ask for succor from us or the Rovers. We must send a new message to the Senate to advise this. Perhaps an escort to be sure they do not stray if all is not honest?"

"Would your Senate not take offense if the Cadre escorted these people onto your lands?

This woman would be of interest to our Queen. As you are not at war with Fredric we may not say what you should do with these people. But we would be wary in your place. Taking them inside Stara or any of your villages could be very dangerous. Giving us custody may spare your people trouble. See what your Senate says to this. We will escort them here as you request. It is only a matter of a few miles to take them to our outpost if your Senate decides."

Hai bowed again.

"I, I am asking this of you, for escort I mean. There are now mines in the pass and the report says there are children. I would not see them harmed, but I fear the tagudal may come and my friends left two fighters short, if your Cadre brothers journey with the refugees."

Before Strike could comment, QuickStep piped up from the ledge.

"Children? Strike we must go. It is not safe for children. Besides the FreeSouls would have to go on foot and that would take hours. We could have them all back in time for evening meal. They are probably very poorly if the reports are true. Hungry and probably ill too."

Strike gave QuickStep a long look, which she returned with just a touch of irritation in her face. He rolled his eyes and turned back to Hai.

"We go to escort refugees. Warn the outpost. We will not be shot by nervous guardians. We will do no harm to anyone unless they are less than honest about their intent."

"That is well enough and I thank you, for the children." Hai bowed once more and rushed off to send his messages.

Strike dismounted and secured his saddle. He rubbed the ears of his Pegasor. It was better to do than remain still. We are bored and whenever we are bored, well. He sighed and his brother's laughter echoed within his head. Strike graced him with a scowl which amused Shadow further.

Shadow's Pegasor padded down the trail, Shatter and QuickStep's already ahead of him, just as relieved to have something to do. Behind him Strike queried Raze as to her intentions and got a snort in reply. Shadow's eyes lit with mirth. Raze would probably trail along at a distance hoping for some misadventure to occur. However he was sure there would be no killing for the little mad one today.

She needs wait until they entered Haven to end Fredric.

The twelve lost to the battlefield called for vengeance. Overwhelmed by sheer numbers they had killed all their foes and honored the Cadre. The empty spaces inside ached from the loss. MeekBlade was trainer before King. First to allow union, to welcome them. Like mind, Cadre. Acceptance. Home. Full.

\*\*\*

At first Casper believed he was seeing things. He even rubbed his eyes after adjusting the magnifier to maximum. People were coming out of the forest in wagons and headed for the pass. He waited, and counted two wagons cramped with dusty ill looking women and children. A third wagon appeared full of household goods. Six men, armed with swords and bows rode horses, driving about ten head of shorthorns before them. Two calves paced beside one of the big horned oxen pulling the wagons. Jumping to his feet Casper rushed out to tell everyone about the party. The Cadre were immediately suspicious of so many mounted men, but held themselves in check. This was the FreeSoul's business and they needed to stay out of it. Scout and Reaper withdrew into the rocks across the pass indicating their neutrality. This end of the canyon was all FreeSoul territory.

\*\*\*

Cherish lay on the rocky ground beneath a wagon wrapped in blew. The FreeSoul outpost was not equipped with extra rations to feed all her people. However, the men did offer strong cups of hot tea and meat pies for the children. Permission was granted to rest while they secured permission for the refugees to proceed along the pass. The FreeSoul called Casper had inquired of their business. Regardless of the submissive stance that had been trained into her, Cherish knew she must speak up for her people. She explained who she was and what they had left behind. She was willing to barter for a cave in the pass for the winter or a place among the FreeSoul themselves, until it was safe to return to her estate.

Caspar and the other guardians had withdrew to discuss it. This was news that must be shared right away. It was further proof that Fredric's plans were all awry. It was possible to end the debate of whether arms should be taken up against him. Emrah remained too weak from his wounds to be moved back to Stara. It would just take time Healer Kameko had insisted. So they kept him warm and waited.

Now the daughter of this mad man was asking for sanctuary. Caspar knew the Cadre would be most upset at this turn of events. But he went off to send the messenger bird to the next post. Hai was nearly an elder. He would know what to do.

Cherish was startled by Joseph's shout. She scrambled out to see what was wrong and froze in surprise. Her men at arms were visibly shocked and frightened.

She stared, fascinated, as two black armored individuals sat astride giant feathered creatures, the like of which she had never imagined. Their mounts were very white, a brilliant color that stood out against the grey brown mountain. She wondered why they were so when everything else on Nadredd could hide itself. Even most horses and cattle were brown or black. The wind stirred what appeared to be feathers of the creatures mane and tail. Cherish thought they were meant to be horses, but something went wrong. She had never seen faces like these. The wide golden eyes looked like messenger birds. Large round furry ears were disarming. Then one of them yawned. Long fangs and very sharp teeth startled everyone. She quailed to think what it must eat as big as it was. There were shades of grey stripped in its coat. Every time the creatures growled or hissed her men would twitch in agitation. But kept their hands up, far from the swords they wore. These were Pegasors, the creatures that defied logic. Seasons ago men were branded liar or demented when attempting to describe them.

The man and woman intrigued her. Their eyes were hard, their faces partially obscured by the odd helms they wore. Hands remained resting on their weapons. The blasters looked new. Caspar rushed down from the building above them waving his hands in a calming gesture toward her group. He did not attempt to get closer to the pair. He explained what was happening.

The riders stirred when they heard Fredric was her father and the creatures grumbled. She had begged at minimum succor for the children through the winter.

So now they waited for the messenger bird to return with an answer. Caspar questioned her further, about the tagudal. She advised that she had not seen anything, but that the snake population had increased near her estate so much they had to burn them out. That with the information that the forest to the north was bare of any game at all set an ominous tone. The guardians admitted among themselves to be glad the Cadre was there with the more formidable blasters.

Eventually things settled down and the Cadre woman climbed up to the cave. Cherish went back to her blankets. So much could still go wrong.

She fell asleep.

Was awake in the first moment Joseph shook her shoulder. The messenger bird had returned with instructions for them to wait for a Cadre escort to take them to the next outpost. Joseph was very upset. They were being put in the hands of demons. The FreeSoul's did not know if their government would allow the refugees to stay. He was very frightened they would be imprisoned or worse. Cherish assured him that she would stand up for everyone's desire to remain together. Maybe they could be confined to the pass for the winter if the FreeSouls would not allow the group to live with them.

Joseph turned away, practically wringing his hands in agitation. He was startled out of his revery by the Cadre female.

"I am Reaper. Your escort will be Cadre, however your party will be handed over to the FreeSouls. We have no interest in having adults in our territory who hate and fear us as much as you do. Mind your manners and all will be well."

Joseph found himself only able to nod. The woman was of a height and the armor was dark as the pitch. Such a horrible name. It still amazed him that the Cadre allowed women proud of welding a sword and killing. Demons indeed to breed such females.

Reaper looked over his shoulder at the blonde woman who said she was Fredric's daughter. From the look of her, life with father had been as hellish as it was for the retainers that huddled in the wagons. She had passed along some of her own rations to the FreeSouls, figuring this lot would not accept food directly from her. Scout and tossed in some of his precious quinoa biscuits for the children.

They were made with a thick sharp cheese from one of Baron Meinrad's farms. Scout hoarded the things like precious metals whenever they appeared in the mess.

Reaper stepped around the man. He tensed up but the blonde waved him back.

Close up it was hard to remember this was a woman. Cherish wondered if the armor was padded. She could not remember ever seeing a woman built like this.

"It is possible my Queen would wish to speak to you. I do not know for certain. But if you accept a place with the FreeSouls, we will not force the issue."

"I cannot tell you much of his plans. I have been away from home since my sixteenth summer. My husband thought me safer never to visit again. I know his servants are worse off than my own people. I know his criminals have taken everything. Many fled to the wastelands. They preferred death there than to remain and watch their women violated and sons and husbands killed in this senseless war."

Cherish was held under that sharp gaze for a long moment before the woman gave her a curt nod and walked away.

Scout rode out for a while, concerned of what kind of reception the twins would get. He did not want these people to panic. They were on the ragged edge. Reaper considered the refugees needed to remain cowed. She had no desire to be putting panicked men to the sword in front of their children. The idea was disgusting. So she paced. Frightened adults and fascinated children watched.

Mason pushed them hard the morning after finding the estate empty. It was easy to see their passage. He was sure they were headed for the pass and hoped to catch them. They were closing in when Mason consider his reception. He had pretty much never gave Cherish a thought other than the day she was handed off to Eustace. One less mouth to feed. There was rabble to be trained and supplies to be collected. He would send men or he would come with them, get what he needed and leave. Sometimes he would see her. She looked fed and clean. Nothing else was of interest.

The men at arms of Eustace had placed his body in a wagon and took him home. In retrospect Mason could acknowledge their loyalty to their master, even admire it. He suspected no one stopped to see if Luthor was alive.

His useless attempts to rally the men still drove him nearly mad with rage, yet at the same time, he had been as frightened as they. Two demons stood back to back and laughed as they cut his men down. That infernal hair of theirs actually snatched men off their feet and held them for the slaughter. Manson would not admit to cowardice. But those images remained through the pitch, smothering him, unable to wake.

Now he was attempting, what? A reconciliation? No. No he truly could not see that happening even if she was the only family left alive. There was no reason for Cherish to even acknowledge him. Well standing here staring at the mountainside was accomplishing nothing. Mason looked over his shoulder at Daniel, quiet yet attentive, his eyes unwavering on Mason. Make the FreeSouls understand Daniel was not a soldier, just a boy half-starved and in need of food and rest like all the other servants on their way to this pass.

Mason checked his saddle and tightened the cinch. Brute was tossing his head, anxious to be moving. Sword in easy reach the man and the silent boy proceeded into the pass.

Joseph and Cherish stood shoulder to shoulder in front of the wagons loaded once again with their people. She felt unattached to what was happening. She never imagined, not even when she saw the strange Pegasors and a woman who was a soldier. Not even when she understood the FreeSouls feared Cadre as much as her people did. She never imagined.

Cherish never imagined they would be . . . beautiful. Reaper's companion returned. Directly after him, another female and a really big man had ridden into view. Alert eyes scanned the cliff sides and the positions of their compatriots. The woman was especially vigilant, it seemed, because she rode within a few feet of everyone at the wagons to look them over. She took particular note of Joseph and the other men.

The FreeSouls had demanded their weapons before the new party arrived. Joseph wanted to argue, but Casper explained they wanted nothing to put the Cadre on edge. If her people were no threat their weapons would be unnecessary.

And then another shock, leaving everyone gaping. Twins, as if one looked into a glass at himself. Their eyes were large and gold as CatsEye on a clear night. Long red brown hair actually sparkled with fiery highlights. But it was their faces that arrested her. Their features seemed to blend into some level of perfection she could not describe. Strange, but beyond handsome. Cherish had never seen a man of Haven who could come near to this in appearance. But, some instinct raised the fine hairs on her body. Her heart was attempting to run away from her breast. Dangerous did not come close to describing them.

Ignoring everyone, the men went directly to Reaper. Cherish heard the startled consternation behind her when that beautiful hip length hair leapt into the air, curled around

Reaper's head and threaded beneath her helm. A few moments of tense silence and the two slipped away from her riding toward the refugees. One of them addressed Cherish.

"We are Strike and Shadow. We will escort you to the next outpost. The Senate of the FreeSouls should have advised what is to be done with you. The pass is mined with explosive all along its length. That is why we are sent. FreeSouls fear injury to your young who are naturally without caution. We go now."

The Gifted turned and headed away without looking back.

"I am QuickStep. You will follow me. Keep to the very center of the pass. Understand this. If I believe that anyone of you has intent to harm the Gifted. I will cut you down without hesitation."

Just as QuickStep wheeled her mount away from Cherish a shout went up from the lookout.

In seconds Reaper's Pegasor had leapt into the rocks and the unknown rider was shadowed in the lee of the cliff side with the other woman.

Every head turned in startled bewilderment, too disconcerted by the last few minutes. It was not long before Casper was once again on the ground with three of the other guardians at his back.

Cherish could not help her gasp of surprise to see her father's prized stallion gallop into the passage, pawing the air as he came to a stop before the FreeSouls.

"Mason!"

How was this possible? Had someone betrayed them all?

Cherish felt faint with fear.

He sat astride with all the arrogance she had come to associate with him. He was heavily armed. When her mind began to stagger back into motion, she wondered what the Cadre would do. Here was the man who lead the attack on Daear. Surely the Cadre would kill him.

"What are you, you doing?"

"I came looking for you sister mine."

"No, no no. I will not stay in Haven and starve to death. I will not let these people be stripped of what little is left by father's madness! You!"

Cherish felt the tears fall and flushed with anger. How he dare come to return her home like a sack of potatoes.

"I did not come to get you Cherish. I wanted to find out if you would be willing to leave for your own safety. Father intended to marry you off to one of those scum. He wanted your estate stripped of whatever food you had to feed them. Roddy is dead and all the men who rode with him. A tagudal, one of your people said."

Mason looked to Casper has he spoke. His eyes had taken in the sheer terror on the faces of the refugees and the guardians were shifting restlessly, eyes sliding left and right. He alone with a boy at his back could not be the reason for this fear. The men at arms were actually sweating in the cool air.

"What else has happened? Why are you so . . . "

"We are why man of Haven. We are why."

Mason was struck speechless as the twins appeared around the bend. Demons! He could do nothing but stare at the lifted hair stirring around their heads like a cloud.

"We know you man of Haven. We know you." Coils caught the scent and fear from the leader of the army that fought them. Strike and Shadow would not forget him. They were assured of his identity by scent and sound.

Mason went for his sword when QuickStep, with Shatter at her back, came into view much too close to his sister. Casper's blaster knocked him from the saddle. Daniel yelled in protest, but went quiet when the Reaper's sword nicked his chin.

"There will be no more violence here!" Casper's voice rose over the tumult of frightened servants and the angry bugle of Brute dancing over the body of his former rider.

"Please let me take care of Brute. Please do not hurt him. I am his handler, please let me. I have no weapons I swear!"

"Calm the beast down, so we can confine your master. Any tricks will get you killed boy."

Daniel leaped from the saddle and his demeanor changed instantly. With soft voice and gentle movements he approached the prancing stallion. It took more than a few moments before Brute stood trembling under his hand.

"Please, please listen. Mason saved me, he drugged his father and the men. He helped us get away. The others have the Master's horses and all the food they could take. They are coming here. Please we only want peace. Mason saved us. We were starving. Master gave all the food to the soldiers and his friends. Mason saved us. I swear it is the truth, I swear it!"

"These things will not be discussed now. Remember this is FreeSoul land. No one has authority here but me as commander of this outpost." Casper's voice was firm, even if his face was sweaty and eyes wide. He held the blaster firmly.

"Now, the Queen of Daear has reasonable issues with this man. He will be shackled by my people and given to you, Gifted of Daear, to be turned over to your authorities. He will not be murdered or abused in anyway. If you will not agree to this I will have him sent to the Senate for consultation with your General and the Queen. You will escort these people as agreed. When or if other refugees arrive we will notify the outposts for escort by our people. I am sure you wish to return to your city quickly with this captive."

Casper searched the faces of the Cadre, who seemed arrested by his forceful speech. The Cadre could guess or sense what he felt, standing up to the demons that he feared more than anything.

Reaper gave the FreeSoul a very rare smile. Scout could only stare in surprise. Casper had always been tentative around them. Now he stood braced for trouble, the blaster pointedly aimed into the dirt, but easily lifted into action if needed. Impressed, Scout grinned.

Casper resented the smile on Reaper's face. It was the smile of an approving parent. He felt himself scowl, an expression rare for him.

QuickStep kept her eye on the twins. Shatter kept his eye on the sister and her people. For too long a moment the tableau held.

"It will be as you say FreeSoul. We will take the one called Mason to our Queen. We will take the people to the outpost. We will take the leader of murderers to our Queen."

The twins turned away once more and moved from sight. Their eerie sing-song, double speech usually signified excitement or anger. Anger was without a doubt now. The remaining Cadre looked to Casper.

"Pello, Wali bind him quickly and very secure please. We cannot afford any attempts to escape and the Cadre kill him. He must face justice for his crimes. Take him."

Casper gestured to Scout, but it was Shatter that stepped forward and checked the bindings, then stripped the body of weapons. He lifted Mason, walked back to his Pegasor and tossed Mason's body over the rump of the beast. The big head turned to watch as her dominant secured the body with clamps hanging from the saddle rings. The Pegasor sniffed and growled baring her fangs. Shatter thumped his baby on the shoulder and she snapped at him in irritation. Shatter climbed in the saddle and disappeared around the bend after the twins.

"Come on you lot. Follow me like before. Make no attempt to approach the prisoner. You are responsible for your own lives. Move!" QuickStep's admonishment got the frightened souls moving.

Reaper spoke to Daniel as he stood overwhelmed by events.

"You boy. Follow behind this lot, but do not fall behind. Stay to the middle of the pass so you do not get blown up by the explosives. Keep your stallion well away from the Pegasors. He will want to challenge as you can see. They like meat too much to ignore him if he draws blood, otherwise they will give him no mind. You have nothing to fear from us child. The one you call Mason is to answer, and his father if we ever get our hands on him. You will get your chance to speak to our Queen about what happened in Haven. She is about your age. She will listen. Now get going."

Daniel heard every word. The demon Queen would

BENEATH CATSEYE         173

speak to him? The thought nearly gave him heart failure and he reeled with sudden dizziness. Reaper's armored arm caught before he sagged to the ground.

"Breath child. There now, just breath. You are very underfed."

Reaper talked Daniel back to consciousness. A FreeSoul was bending over him as well, holding a cup of hot liquid to his mouth. Daniel took a tentative sip. Spicy, some kind of flavored tea. He eventually had his own hands around the cup and experienced acute upset when it was empty. When he looked up everyone else was gone.

"Once you are set to rights I will take you to catch up with your people. Take this moment to adjust to all that has occurred. It would make anyone faint." He heard the Cadre woman say.

Then there was a wondrous scent and a little bit of warm pastry was slipped in his mouth. What bliss, he could not remember. There was a light crust that crunched between his teeth, warm gravy and meat. He did not care what it was. For a while he just rested there, chewing when it was placed in his mouth. The world righted itself when he was able to sit unsupported and bite into the meat pie. Reaper kept him from bolting it down, then there was another cup of spicy tea.

He was feeling much more himself when he finally mounted up. Reaper lead him down the pass until they saw the back of the slow moving wagons. She allowed him to touch her Pegasor as they walked along. The creature was a marvel. The thick layer of tiny feathers mixed with soft fur, but the mane feathers were needle sharp amid the fluff. Daniel gave this woman a long stare and looked ahead to the other servants.

No one that he could remember ever treated him with such care before. And she consorted with demons, but showed them no deference and no fear. She sat in the saddle with the assurance he had only seen in others like her and Mason. Daniel thought. Looked at Reaper again as she moved ahead. Perhaps, well maybe, if he was not punished for being from Haven. Maybe he could find a place. Someone had to take care of the giant beasts and he knew from gossip around the estate that the demons had horses just like his people. Yes, there could be a place for him. He would get a life without fear, without hunger. He would get it with the demons. Squaring his shoulders, Daniel rode on.

\*\*\*

Mason should be back at any moment. Fredric stood on the walkway watching the horizon for sign of his son. Together they would torture the traitorous scum into submission.

He woke this morning to find the house silent and the bedroom fire smoldering. There were no sounds of animals anxious to be milked, or his stallion's whinny. He felt lethargic and wondered if he was coming down with something. His head ached. The sound of his own footfalls were muffled one moment, then banging in his ears like an anvil. He managed the walk to his office and grabbed the blaster from his desk drawer. Whatever the hell was going on, someone would pay for their neglect.

Then there was shouting and screaming. He rushed to

the front hall. When he flung the door back, weak sunlight stabbed him in the eyes like a knife. He staggered out only to be assaulted by a hysterical crowd of supporters and soldiers.

Angry did not begin to describe it. The adrenaline wiped the fog from his mind. He fired the blaster above the heads of the mob. The blast hit one the men who was flung back. The noise ceased.

"Now, what the hell is the meaning of this."

Finley gulped and grit his teeth. He had been vomiting since the wee hours of the pitch. He did not think he had much time. The cramps were worse, and there was blood.

"There are dead men in the barracks. The rest of us are sick, some dying even now. The damned servants poisoned us all and ran off."

"All of them Fredric, all of them!" ranted Lewis, still insulted that Mason had spat at his feet the day before.

"They kidnapped my Jemma. I want her back. How could this happen? We all could be dead in our beds!"

"My house is empty. All the meat and bread taken. The last of my sweet bread. The last!"

"The very blew off my bed is gone. I woke from the cold. They were gone, everyone gone!"

"The guards, where the hell are the guards?" Fredric demanded of the now doubled over gasping soldier.

"Stunned in the post house! No horses, no ox found . . . "

Finley began to vomit right there, dropping to his knees and unable to speak again. He collapsed in the unending stream of blood and bile. A few of his other men were holding each other up. Some drooled, the others were clutching at their stomachs, sweating and trembling. They were barely standing.

"You lot get back to the barracks. This will have to run its course. There is no cure except your own strength. Now go!" Fredric ignored the expressions of shock and terror on their faces. A few staggered off hoping to make it to their beds again. Two more dropped to the ground vomiting until they lost consciousness.

Loud exclamations and questions once more assaulted his ears from the supporters that were proving themselves completely useless in a crisis.

"So the servants have poisoned us and run. None of you thought to see how I fared? You pathetic excuses did not take up arms to go get them? They were still in walking distance at dawning. What reason do I keep you alive if you serve no purpose! Mason will meet them on the way and they will return with their tail between their legs. Then I will execute them for treason along with you! Get to the post house and untie those idiots. When they wake up they can clean up behind the others."

Fredric shoved his way passed the crowd and hurried to the barn. He flung open the doors. The wan light did not allow him an illusion of animals in the stalls. His gaze settled on what should be the prize stallion he had spent rotations breeding. Gone. They dared take what was his!

His walked to the barracks. Men lay in the yard. Most appeared dead. Some were crawling as blood dribbled from their mouths. Where would the scum get pydru? It was made from venoms and noxious plants. There was not a cure for it. If you survived, you were never the same afterward. He did not bother going in. They would recover or not, and he had no time for the weak willed.

Mason would make them pay for this. The men he usually took to gather supplies were few, but they were the best at arms. The idiot servants would have no chance.

Fredric walked through the barren kitchen garden and into the kitchen door of his home. There was nothing but a few scoops of flour left in the bins. No dried meat, no journey bread. Nothing.

Mason would make them pay for their temerity. He walked through the empty house and out the front door. He ignored the helpless idiots still milling around. Fools could not wipe their own asses without a servant. Perhaps he would make them clear the bodies and sweep the courtyard. The entry to his ancestral hall must continue to be pristine for the arrival of his subjects. People were not impressed by leaders appearing the least bit slovenly. Fredric remained on the walkway long after CatsEye was obscured by new rain clouds, boiling up purple and green.

# Reprisal

Coils! There was nothing left to vomit. But Mason heaved anyway as the Pegasor leaped over another boulder and another. The cursed beast seemed able to run nonstop day and night. Had they been traveling day and night? He was blinded by something that sealed his eyes shut. His wrists were clamped together, attached to chains. Something tethered him to the saddle by his waist. He pounced against thick jutting backbone. His body slid back and forth as the beast moved. They went up and down and up, up and down and . . .

Why would they not kill him?

Mason first woke to pitch, searing pain in his head and nausea. Damn blaster packed a bunch like an anvil. There were voices, but the sounds made little sense. He was locked in the pitch and kept speechless by his abused stomach. Would the beast never grow tired? Coils, he was sure a few ribs were cracked.

\*\*\*

Daniel look on with trepidation as the Pegasor leapt up one side of the cliff. Ran a good distance, only to spin and leap back down to the trail. Surely Mason was being hurt by all that leaping about.

Mason's sister and her people had been left behind, this morning. Cherish had given him feed for the horses and the FreeSouls and provided water. He had kept his mouth shut as he was fed by guardians of the outpost last night and again this morning. He was so grateful for those meat pies. He hardly remembered the last time he ate anything so thick with meat and there were vegetables too.

The one called QuickStep sat and talked to him after everyone ate. She did not seem very stern or grim when she told him what was to come. He had been reminded of the facts. The facts as they were did not make for a long life expectancy for Mason. Yes, he had saved the servants, but was he not the reason they went hungry in the first place? Did he not gather the food and guard it? Were people beaten for stealing it? Had people been executed for stealing food they desperately needed? Did he do his father's bidding by forcing people from their homes, stealing their food and clothes for the army? Did he not force them to fight and execute them if they resisted? Should he not pay for his crimes?

Daniel was weeping by the time the woman relented. She sat beside him while he cried himself out. How could he have forgotten these things? His father had gone with the army full of confidence that success would bring them the right to return to their home. The riches of the demons would be theirs. All the sacrifice, the suffering would be worth it in the end. Yes Fredric was a harsh master, but the demons were such terrors everyone had to be strong and sacrifice for the greater good. Daniel would see when he returned victorious and they rode together through the streets of Daear, demons crushed beneath their feet.

Only he did not return. Victory was a joke of wounded, terrified men babbling about demons and pitch clad murderers chasing them through the pitch. Fredric allowed no one time to grieve or retrieve the dead. They must heal quickly and strike fast. The demons would not be expecting their return. Victory was at hand. Men continued to die from their wounds. There were only ill equipped servants for assistance. Seasons past the last healers of Haven fled into the waste with the deserters. Fredric had begun to condemn some of their practices as weakening the people. So the survivors of the battle on the plain continued to expire.

Daniel hung his head in remorse. Because Mason had set him free, he thought him the hero. He was strong and good with his weapons. He rode like one part of the horse. No one on the estate had ever beaten him in a fight. How could he forget that Mason and his father was the cause of so much devastation, for the complete ruin of his own life? He did not speak again to anyone. He was shamed.        Daniel did not look again at Mason tossed around on the back of the Pegasor. He rode along in silence, stripped of his momentary delusion and so very confused. The dawn had risen on him thinking about a future among the demons that killed his father.

This pitch would find him wracked with self-hatred and anguish for wanting a future free from these burdens. Were his father's beliefs wrong? He was dead. But the demons had been kind to Daniel. They had not ridden down from their mountain to attack his people. He knew this much was true. Most of his people thought demons were legend until that day on the battlefield. But if they existed then the old stories had to be true. The bad military people and the scientists were long dead, before Daniel's grandfather and even before that. If the demon continued to make monsters why had they not come before to raid Haven's people? Fredric had done that and worse. Daniel found no peace under the clouded sky, his thoughts continued as pitch as the vista he stared into.

QuickStep felt badly. She had not allowed the boy to keep that sad gaze upon the hero of his past few dawns. It was an almost conditioned response. The boy had suffered long term and one act of kindness, not matter how off hand, created a supporter for the murderous bastard. The boy needed to be clear in his own head. She had observed his worshipful gaze on Reaper when they caught up with the party. The child was just too vulnerable. Now he was burdened with doubts. Which was much better than being a mindless husk drifting along like llygredd, subject to changing alliances with every new association. Whether he remained in Daear or returned to Haven, he must be his own man not manipulated by anyone. Still she felt really bad about what she did. That night she would sleep wrapped tightly in coils between Strike and Shadow when their turn at watch ended.

\*\*\*

Shatter fed and watered the prisoner. The loss of his twelve brothers and sisters ate at him like llyncas on a muskie calf. He had never wanted to kill someone more than this scum. But he had given oaths of fealty to BrightLance, driven by fierce heartache and blood lost. Once again a Cadre warrior sat on the throne of Daear. He would be loathed to disappoint his little Queen and deny her justice. So he took off the chains and checked the man for injuries. Shatter had no remorse over the darkening bruises across the man's torso. Tomorrow he would be chained behind Shatter's baby and be forced marched to his end. It would save the scum from further damage until the General got hold of him. Thoughts of what Mason would suffer at the hands of BareBlade comforted him during his night watch.

***

Raze was disgruntled. No one was foolish enough to stalk their back trail away from the border. The twins had been smart to avoid their own outposts. She was sure the guards would even take up arms against them to satisfy their need for vengeance. It was all of little mind to her. The Queen must perform for all of Daear now, instead of her Cadre uncles and aunts. Raze would have just tortured the man to death, very slowly of course.

But other humans needed to feel they were justified when killing. At least that was her understanding of the others. Soon enough they would go after Fredric. Then she may find the necessary close work and momentary satiation. Still it was ill done, that no one followed them, so she could instruct them regarding their poor choices in life. When did prey get so intelligent?

Raze sniffed in irritation and mounted up to return to the night camp. Perhaps someone would spar with her come dawn to work some of this energy off. She had never killed a Cadre member yet. Every one of them knew Raze was insane. It did not bother her that they did. Living with her kept them sharp. Excellent killers every one of them. She wondered if she felt pride. How disconcerting. With one last look at scattered clouds beginning to build, Raze turned back to camp. They needed to beat the next rainstorms home. It would be a misery to travel across the plains in driving rain. She would really want to kill someone then.

\*\*\*

BareBlade had finished up his work for the day and secured his office door. The scents from the galley were tantalizing. His stomach grumbled just as every coiled Cadre walking along the corridor turned to the shadowed recess that hid the bottom of the ramp. Something flew into the hall and smacked into the opposite wall. BareBlade's sword came to hand as the same time the others rushed down the hall with their weapons drawn. Suddenly the twins appeared from the dark, hair floating around them both. Raze, Shatter and QuickStep appeared at their backs.

We have him BareBlade, we have the one who leads. We have him, we have him."

The four Cadre in the hall with the General stared at the unconscious figure against the wall. On closer look it was a man. He stank. Brace moved forward cautiously until he realized the man was manacled and unconscious. He attempted to ascertain the identity of the reeking body. Brace looked up at BareBlade as the twin's coils enveloped the man, advising events in the swiftest manner possible. He twitched more than once at the intrusion of his mind, but the general had a number of rotations to adjust to the twins preferred reporting method. BareBlade's glee and satisfaction ignited the twins and their emotional response to his praise for bringing the prisoner back alive drew the attention of more than one Cadre member, so the hall began to fill.

"Get to interrogation and prep the strongest serum. Strip him, have a healer look him over. I will be coming in to question him immediately after I advise the Queen. A fortunate day, very fortunate."

BareBlade disappeared into the dark stairwell and sped up the ramp. Brace and Sticker dragged Mason swiftly along the hall by his ankles. No one appeared to note Lucan, dumbfounded, remaining in the center of the hallway. The twins, Shatter, and QuickStep rushed to shower off the grime of travel and treat themselves to some real home cooked food. Raze went to clean her weapons.

On the decks below Daniel watched with huge eyes as the squires unsaddled grumbling Pegasors and brushed them down. It was a quick job. The Pegasors were hungry for the dearhart which were already racing in panic around the enclosure. The children dragged him off to show him a place to stable Brute. Before his head stopped spinning Daniel was eating in the squire barracks and sleeping in clean sheets and warm blew.

\*\*\*

Mason choked on the mucus and bile running from his nose and mouth. He could not see or breath. Panic began to override his ability to appear unmoved by the injections and his cramping stomach. He thought someone said he was allergic to the drug before his dark world became overwhelmed with the anvil that slammed into his chest.

More hands clamped around his arms when he began to writhe desperate for air. He attempted to break free from those bruising hands but found himself rising in the air and body slammed onto some surface. His legs flailed and his head banged repeatedly against metal. He was dying. Something hot pierced his chest and his spine bowed with the sudden influx of fiery air. He managed to gasp and could not stop tears or the trembling. He filled his lungs with hot precious air until the flashing lights faded to pitch.

Later Mason realized he was alone lying in urine and feces. He managed to roll to one side and pressed his face into the floor. He was insensible for who knows how long when hands were back and the scent of some astringent cleaning fluid turned his stomach again. Rough cloth was being applied to his genitals and legs. When he attempted to move away from the icy water, others clamped down on his arms again pinning him in place. He kicked out and a huge hand encircled his throat and clamped down. No no no no. Mason forced his body still and the hand stopped squeezing. Someone raised his legs in the air and his backside was scrubbed. He could not stop the twitch in protest of this humiliation and his throat was squeezed shut again. They left as suddenly as they had come.

Cool water pushed into his mouth. Dragged, lifted, then slammed into a chair. Legs curled up in reaction to stomach churning pain. He bit his tongue when his testicles were crushed against the metal. A sound like air escaping the room caused him to twitch in panic.

Another injection. Mason jumped from the chair, or tried to. Hands pressed him down until the skin on his back was raw. Whatever they injected this time burst into his veins with scalding heat and he lost his breath again. Panic made his body shiver and his feet drummed the floor in reaction to an immense adrenaline rush. Light spun in nauseating swoops, stability abandoned.

The General pulled the prisoner up by his hair after injecting the altered drug in the prominent jugular vein. He stepped back and watched the man lose all control, flailing and scuttling around the floor until he found the corner and cowered there. Astounding to find the drug had such an affect. Who could have guessed an allergic reaction to something in the food would be compounded by a further reaction to the antidote. It took no time for BareBlade to have a drug replicated to reproduce the physical effects the prisoner had suffered. Adding a hallucinogenic meant fists and blades would be unnecessary to get their information. Colby had proved resistant to physical threat and did not have any useful intelligence after the effort.

Thinking of that braggart scum bought a wide grin to BareBlade's visage. The loudmouth and his companions were shoveling muskie shit for the fertilizer plant for the remainder of their lives. BrightLance also condemned the rabble to live with the muskie bulls, tending them and bagging waste. They were denied filters to block the concentrated odor in the barns and wore tracking collars to make sure they stayed put. They had to eat and sleep in the same shelters as the animals. Showers were a privilege earned. If they were not careful and solicitous the bulls would make short work of them. Most entertaining.

Now the General would sit back and listen. Somewhere in the incoherent raving and fantasy would be glimmers of the truth. When the prisoner was worn down by his physical reactions and terrors, BareBlade would have his system cleansed and then question him. His questions would be readily answered.

Mason babbled traitorous fears. Every disdainful impression expressed. Survival of the purges. Executing seditious families, so he would not join their fate. Survival more important than ideologies he was taught. So he killed when ordered and beat his father's rabble into enough shape to take the field and die. Facing the inevitability of death every day. Only foes for company. No value, a tool for father's delusions. Eaten alive by the tagudal! Run run run! The demons had her! Kill . . . A starving boy who obeyed. Bloody sheets with a whimpering blue newborn . . .

Mason raved through the dark. The demons returned and tore him apart. He could not stop them. He could not stop them and his heart and will failed as he strangled. Coward, coward . . .

"I have many questions and you are the man with the answers. Of course you could relive the last two dawnings again. We have a large supply of the toxin."

The captive trembled. Oh yes, BareBlade would know

everything.

***

Floor to ceiling double paned windows encircled the bright winter throne room at measured intervals. Across the circular floor, footsteps would be muffled by hexagon shaped mini tiles in alternating shades of pale blue and a slightly deeper yellow. The walls were also a soft nearly translucent wash of white, yellow and blue. The solar cells provided light in this room during the stormy dawn.

Right now the windows were covered by low lying clouds which reflected the room's light. The effect was of silver curtains blocking the view. Water spout shaped columns of white ceramic vases were filled with green fern and a variety of yellow blossoms. The flower pots anchored three arched entrances into the room. Smaller wall scones, spilled lush green ivy to the floor between the windows. It was a clean refreshing sight to relieve the endless days of rain and gloom.

Plush seating groups were scattered about. Before one of the windows Mila was updating the computer security system in the armrests of the Fleet Admiral's chair. The metal frame of the chair had been carefully maintained. Only the color and fabric varied, matching the ever changing décor of the winter and summer throne rooms. It was as close as the Daear had to a throne. Fleet Admiral Pryor's office chair preserved through the centuries, and no one allowed to sit in but the Kings.

Standing beneath an archway into the room, BrightLance thought it was nonsense. But just like her crown, the ladies insisted she sit in it whenever she used the rooms.

She did admit to herself it was an extremely comfortable chair to rest in. She was hard pressed to remain awake during the more tiresome days making idle conversation with courtiers. It would not due for BrightLance to snuggle into that wondrous support and take a nap, but oh the temptation.

However, today would not be idle. The full Council would be present in this room including the lessor Baronets. The Cadre would escort Mason Brooks to be displayed before them before he was sentenced to life confined in the muskie pens. She had considered harsher measures, even death. However that fine line the people walked could not be ignited by spilling his blood in a public execution. He would not be a martyr to the cause of Daear's extermination or have his death ignite blood lust in the whole of her people. For a man so proud, this would be unbearable humiliation. It would have to do until Fredric was detained. BrightLance hoped the mad coil still lived. Fredric was the source of these deluded men who wrecked such havoc on her people. He would be executed, insane or not. Daear would not house and feed his continued madness.

Since Mason had been incarcerated, BareBlade was insisting on the death penalty. BrightLance had talked to the Council, debated and meditated on what was to become of the so called general. She spent time in the archives pouring over Old Earth history and military records. A viewing of the interrogation only solidified her opposition against the public execution the entire Cadre hungered for. Yes her father was dead, along with her Cadre kin. However, MeekBlade taught her to put the welfare of all the people first. She could not let it be said she was a tool for BareBlade or the Council.

Fourteen dawns had passed since the Citadel issued a statement to advise the citizens of the capture of Colby and his men. BrightLance had been quite surprised when the man laughed uproariously on being advised of his brother's death. She could still find it in her heart to be sad for that poor boy dying, sick and frightened in the dark. The men had been tried quickly after the interrogations. The trials were broadcast at the Bard houses around the valley, if any adult wished to attend. Colby's hate spewed testimony came as no surprise. He had fought that day on the field but knew nothing about the ambush of King and Cadre. Fredric did not trust Colby with secrets, because his tongue was very loose when drunk. He boasted how Mason was probably the brains behind everything, after all he was the only son worthy of Fredric the Great. The man spat at the feet of the lawyer with that statement and said no more.

The Court found two of Colby's men guilty of the willful murder of unarmed servants before they left Haven to spy in the forest. Another one had been an accomplice in the death of a FreeSoul Samaritan. BrightLance advised the Senate that as soon as the weather cleared these would be returned to them and the surviving Havenites for justice. There was little more the Cadre could do now with the winter storms occurring one after the other. Of some concern was the giant tagudal reported headed north, but she was aware it could bypass them or even be diverted onto the plains. It may even hibernate through the winter. It was the least important of her concerns now it was no longer threatening the pass into FreeSoul's territory. No matter its size, if it needed to be killed Daear had the means.

The report of refugees arriving in FreeSoul territory from Haven was good news for her people. They were servants mostly, people press ganged into doing Fredric's will because their parents had believed his father's tales of glory. The FreeSoul's reported they were weakened from hunger and many could not read or write. It had been a slow relentless fall. Their blind belief they could take by force what others had worked for led them to dissolution. The people of Haven had survived much better when they kept their independence and did not follow any leader. She hoped the ones who fled had not fallen victim to Nadredd's cruelty. If they survived maybe they would return from the plains.

She had received more than one dispatch from Stara. The Senate was up in arms over the news that Fredric's men were incapacitated by pydru. It was no great leap to realize the poison could only have been available if it was going to be used against Daear. She was assured that the deadly poison was destroyed in the furnaces FreeSouls used to smelt their ore. She was relieved, BareBlade was skeptical.

BrightLance returned to her quarters. Today would not be a day of revenge but of justice. As her Cadre endured the loss of their King and comrades, Mason would endure rotations of humiliation. The knowledge that he was the one with the strength to put down his father's madness and did not would haunt him. He could have been something more than a follower and a murderer but chose the cowards way out. There was no way to predict what the future could have been if he had taken his brothers under his wing. Farrell most likely would have still suffered or been killed outright. But what ifs always harassed one in the dark. She wanted to think the war would have been avoided and a woman who finally stood up to her husband would not have been locked in a room until she died, disregarded by her sons.

***

Mason stood, legs held slightly apart by a metal bar and manacles around his ankles. His arms were secured at his back in some kind of restrictive wrap with magnetized cuffs on his wrists. They kept him nude. His blood pressure rose and fell so fast BareBlade assigned a Cadre healer to monitor him during his coming audience with the Queen. He was unaware of how many dawnings had come and gone.

For the first time since being captured he was not blind. Two Cadre females anchored him holding the end of bars attached to a metal collar around his neck. The collar stressed him more than anything else. Cannot swallow, cannot exhale cannot live. He twitched when the healer stabbed him with a needle and the artificial calm washed over him. He believed his body would never stop shuddering in reaction to injections and the fearful response each one imposed or quelled.

Mason's head was full of things, real and imagined? He could no longer be sure. There was only fear beneath the artificial light and in the pitch.

A sharp tug on his neck got Mason shuffling down the dim hallway. The catheter tugged and he could not stop the grimace of acute discomfort. A container strapped to his leg grew warm against his skin, as it filled. They had made him watch. Held him down when they put it in. BareBlade was determined no one had to clean up his mess. Mason was almost grateful now, because Cadre lined the walls to watch his progress, some of them with hair unfettered. He could not jerk away as coils skittered across his face and shoulders. It was hard to keep on his feet when his body kept jerking, attempting to avoid the reaching horror.

He could not voice his fear, even if he wanted to. The collar was too restrictive for that. He fell to his knees and the women lifted him by the bars, cutting off his air even more if he did not rise. Struggling up, Mason continued moving where he was guided. Then he saw the demon twins and BareBlade haloed in light. He vision pitched out, but the women dragged him when his feet refused to move anymore. There was nothing he could do to prevent this ending. Surely they were going to be the ones to kill him now.

Confused, Mason stared as the trio was joined by the Cadre female that slept wrapped in their coils. The memory burned through the drug leaving him with an uncontrolled full body tremor. The quartet turned away and he was made to follow them into pitch. A disorienting journey began, up. More shadowed hallways. Head pulled down to see only floor as he was forced along. He tripped through hatches or was lifted over others. His ankles and shins were red from scrapes and forming bruises.

Mason's eyes teared under the searing impact of light and color. The water dried quickly, leaving an irritating itch on his skin. He stared into the room. A few faces seemed familiar and brought to mind the rout on the battlefield. Those faces, full of anger, fierce and frightened.

There were women here, not serving, but talking to these warriors. Mason wondered at it, when women of Haven's duty was birthing babies for the cause and keeping the house. But then demons did things differently. The two that held him seemed as strong as any man he had ever known. He could never forget that screaming monster skewering soldiers either.

Mason's eyes widened, watching a tall woman walk into the room from another archway and sit in a chair before one of the windows. Long brown hair pooled around the chair at her feet when she sat down. She was dressed in a plain grey gown and her expression was grim. She looked across the room into his eyes. Mason could not look away. He tried.

He tried.

He tried.

Another jab of the needle and the shuddering ceased. The prisoner's gaze was released and he was grateful to lower his head. That thin scrape of a woman was the Queen! She was a child!

He no longer felt panic as the few drops of tranquilizer rush through his brain. With a tug on the bars Mason shuffled forward into the bright room. So many eyes looked with surprise upon him. So many with disgust. Mason knew his face was reddened, but even his humiliation was short lived under the drug's domination.

He was jerked to a stop when a loud bang startled everyone in the room. He vaguely realized something had fallen, when a few demons turned away to look at whatever it was. For another long moment he was held suspended off his feet. He guessed the guards were assessing the situation, ready to move him. Perhaps someone did not appreciate his nakedness. His eyes teared up as humor made a fleeting impression before fading as fast it had come. Then he was being pressed to the floor before that chair. Coils! The she devil's hair was cloud over his face and terror left him blank.

A distant hiss voiced his sins inside his head! He wanted so desperately to fight to get away, but he was being held down and there was the voice and nausea and memories. He was vaguely aware when the Queen spoke aloud to the demons in the room. Felt the utter relief when he heard his sentence. Not death, but imprisonment in the muskie pens. He kept his face pressed to the floor as the tears came, ashamed to be relieved he would be humiliated for life instead of executed in the coils of these demons. He took no mind of his present shameful position, naked on the floor before these creatures, his buttocks exposed to the room. Was he a coward all this time, was he?

Then Mason realized there was silence, a physical pressure of quiet. Had he been returned to his cell? His head was snatched from the floor and shook! He squinted under the intense light and stinging pain. A quick impression of a man. Voices suddenly raised, shouting protest. They did want him dead. He knew, he knew it was a trick! His head was shaken again and the man pulled him to his feet. His  was voice demanding, angry yet pleading. Then Mason was pushed to his knees, his hair still wrapped in a vise grip by strong fingers. The hand moved him again until his head rested against the man's body. What was this? What was happening? He jerked when coils once again smothered him, binding him against the man. His heart was determined to leave his chest. He gasped for air that seemed to avoid him.

Consciousness returned and the awareness that he lay on his back looking up at the crowd of people in the room. His

Cadre guards appeared in his line of sight and knelt beside his head. The bars were gone. They kept him pressed against the floor, again. Mason blinked and saw the twins and the other horrors of the battlefield all pressed around him, coils writhing in the air. His terror was suddenly arrested when he made eye contact with a tanned, black haired man. The relief at seeing shorn hair was quickly gone. The eyes were gold but black edged, too painful too painful to look into. He cried out loud. So hungry, so hungry and unfulfilled. Need

   need

   need

   need

   need

   need

   need

   need

   need

Mason found his voice at last. He screamed and he did not stop. Coils of every demon in the room brushed his body, entered his thoughts. Cracked him open like an egg and exposed him, screaming. He fled to the pitch with joy. Did he laugh when he remembered he feared death only moments ago?

   ***

Sleet charged rain beat against the windows and rattled the tiles on the roof. Inside the office of Baron Nardo the frosted, etched glass lamps filled the room with soft white light. The oil, blended with a touch of lavender essence, lent subtle motes to the tranquil atmosphere of the room. The heavy wood desk and chair before the windows was intricately carved with Pegasors leaping in play. The golden brown blew drapes were pulled back to showcase the stormy weather, a sullen contrast to the light and warmth within.

Fire nipped at the logs, flickering in the fireplace on the opposite wall. Two couches, same color as the drapes, were adjacent to it. One long table, with a racing Pegasor engraved on its surface, held a tray with various bottles of liqueurs and tiny glass sipping cups. In rotations past, the bottles were always in various stages of near empty. Today they were topped off and required dusting prior to the Baron having guests. The warm tones of the walls gleamed gold in the firelight. Woven throws of cream, tan and white were tossed over the arms or back of the couches. It was easy to see why the Baron favored his office over other rooms in his household.

The big oak door opened. Mason stepped through. His eyes assessed the area, rechecked the window before he allowed the Baron into the room. He took up his stance at the window looking out onto the horrid weather. Mason would have preferred the muskie pens with his furious brother, where he had been paraded before coming here. Nardo regaled Colby with Mason's new status as Chosen. Colby had spat at Mason and laughed so hard he fell to the ground. He cursed the former proud stallion as a traitor and coward.

Mason had seen the Chosen woman being stroked and petted by the twins. In the days before coming here, he had seen the Queen with her own, a really huge male who made everyone cringe when he walked into a room. The man had stretched under her coils like that Pegasor getting its neck scratched. The thought filled him with despair.

Mason would never be cosseted. The faint memories of his mother, his own passing interest in an obedient stable boy and a brave sister would be all the gentleness he would ever know for the remainder of his days.

\*\*\*

Nardo sat down at his desk and began the tedious task of managing his estate, totally focused on the hand written reports, discs and the palm sized computer. He gave no mind to Mason at his back.

Nardo was enjoying clarity. His secret was secret no longer to the Queen, her immediate council and the Cadre, of course. The others thought he just had the misfortune to find a Chosen amid the enemy of their people. They commiserated with him when he allowed it. The population had been stunned at the revelation, but taking into account the Queen's future husband was a tortured Gifted, they rallied in support. Most thought Farrell had been a fluke. Now they imagined many children tortured and slaughtered.

Nardo truly expected he would be denied, condemned to utter madness and death by his peers. There had never been luck enough to end his pain. He tried his damnedest to get killed so many times. Life had been terror filled since puberty. Faced with the awful realization that there was food all around him he could not consume. Driven by unrelenting hunger he could never satisfy, Nardo was denied the connection to human and Gifted that may have eased his craving. There was residual awareness of his love for family and support of friends, but, they were also food. He was inconsolable and tortured for eighteen nightmarish rotations.

Sitting in the fog of poisonous alcoholic fumes, he was paying no attention to his brothers and the remaining councils filling the room. Mind cleared and focused with an audible snap inside his head. The universe centered on the grimy cowering 'pure' on the floor before his Queen. Nardo remembered little. He came to himself snarling in the ear of the human Mason. He crooned to the human the reality of life from this moment. Mason was his and only his. His to command, his to use.

The human now wore ornamental armor befitting his status as shield for Nardo and any children he may ever have. Mason wore a thin collar of beaten silver etched with the title he now bore, Amddiffynnwr Adfonlon. His brown hair was kept shorn close to his head and his eyes were rarely raised to look directly at anyone considered family or friend of Nardo. The human lived in fear as unrelenting as Nardo's hunger.

The Baron endured the Healers and Baroness Tesni's ruthless pursuit of the reasoning for his 'condition' with rare good humor. They all marveled at his strength of will. Then he returned to his estate near the end of the valley, amid the terraced slopes that ringed it.    He was Llyncu of old surrounded by an abundance of prey.

Nardo applied himself to paperwork with renewed enthusiasm. He was content.

## About the Author

Born in New Orleans, La. and lived in Alexandria until she was twelve, Patricia I. Williams fell in love with Southern California on arrival. She would not want to live anywhere else, at least for this lifetime. She loves knowing the ocean is just beyond the hill and that Disneyland is the happiest place on earth. She enjoys traveling through the Southwest. The history and legends fuel a lot of imaginative Wild West adventures. She loves Science Fiction, film and books. Believes horses, dogs and cats are ideal companions.

Her faith in Jehovah keeps her grounded. She believes one lifetime is not long enough to learn everything. She is wary of all information because it most often is dependent on the good intentions of the provider. These days she finds pleasure is seeing her grandchildren's curiosity about the world around them.

PATRICIA I. WILLIAMS